"*Keeping me here is a joke.*"

"I didn't say it was." That sexy mouth curled as Francisco joined Sarah on the sofa.

"It could be weeks before my father gets your message. And there's no guarantee he'll respond." He really was much too close!

"A man not respond to his daughter's plight?" He wasn't taking her seriously. He moved closer and with a groan of helplessness she slithered toward him, winding her arms around his neck, his mouth so close to hers she could feel the passionate heat of it and savor the kiss that surely had to come...

DIANA HAMILTON is a true romantic, and fell in love with her husband at first sight. They still live in the fairy-tale Tudor house where they raised their three children. Now the idyll is shared with eight rescued cats and a puppy. But despite an often chaotic lifestyle, ever since she learned to read and write Diana has had her nose in a book—either reading or writing one—and plans to go on doing just that for a very long time to come.

Books by Diana Hamilton

HARLEQUIN PRESENTS

Don't miss any of our special offers. Write to us at the following address for information on our newest releases.

Harlequin Reader Service
U.S.: 3010 Walden Ave., P.O. Box 1325, Buffalo, NY 14269
Canadian: P.O. Box 609, Fort Erie, Ont. L2A 5X3

Diana Hamilton
Hostage of Passion

Harlequin Books

TORONTO • NEW YORK • LONDON
AMSTERDAM • PARIS • SYDNEY • HAMBURG
STOCKHOLM • ATHENS • TOKYO • MILAN
MADRID • WARSAW • BUDAPEST • AUCKLAND

RECYCLED PAPER

ISBN 0-373-11804-X

HOSTAGE OF PASSION

First North American Publication 1996.

Copyright © 1995 by Diana Hamilton.

This edition published by arrangement with Harlequin Books S.A.

® and TM are trademarks of the publisher. Trademarks indicated with
® are registered in the United States Patent and Trademark Office, the
Canadian Trade Marks Office and in other countries.

Printed in U.S.A.

CHAPTER ONE

'SOMEONE to see you, Sarah.' Jenny poked her glossy brown head round the inner office door, her pretty face flushed. 'He doesn't have an appointment and he wouldn't give his name.' Her brown eyes turned into saucers. 'I explained that the agency was closed right now and offered to arrange an interview with you tomorrow morning—but he refuses to leave until he's seen you.'

Sarah pushed the last file into the steel cabinet and locked it, a tiny frown on her smooth wide brow as she registered her deputy's agitation. She selected her permanent staff very carefully, paying as much attention to temperament as ability because for the last four years her life had been dedicated to making her secretarial and business agency utterly professional, efficient and highly respected, not only in the North London suburb where it was located but throughout the capital.

Jenny Fletcher had been chosen for her pleasant personality and her calm unflappability but she was unaccountably acting as if she had as much professionalism as a giddy teenager.

Sarah sighed and glanced at her watch. Business had closed for the day twenty minutes ago and she had a dinner date. Nevertheless, even though Scott Secretarial Services wasn't short of clients it went against her policy to turn prospective business away.

'Show him in; I can give him ten minutes,' she instructed, straightening the jacket of her sage-green linen suit as she placed herself neatly on the chair behind her desk, sliding the large leather-bound diary towards her, one fine brow arching quizzically as Jenny gushed breathily,

'I'll sit in, shall I? Take details of his needs.'

Her last word degenerated to an expressive giggle and Sarah's aquamarine eyes went frosty, her voice repressive as she stated, 'That won't be necessary. You may as well go home. I'll lock up.' She wondered again what had got into her normally controlled and perfectly sober assistant and, with deep resignation, decided she knew the answer to that particular question when the most ferociously handsome male she had ever encountered shouldered arrogantly into the room.

Despite the elegantly styled dark business suit there was a raw sexuality, an aura of brooding power about the stranger that few women would be immune to and, in his mid-thirties, she guessed, he would be all too well aware of it. And Jenny, although professional to her fingertips, could be partly excused because she wouldn't have the in-built immunity to such primary masculine magnetism that came completely naturally to her boss.

Sarah gestured to the seat on the opposite side of the desk, gave her usual cool smile and didn't bother to wonder why it felt so forced on this occasion and wasn't surprised when she registered that his voice was dark and smoky, the seductive accent betraying his Spanish birth, because he was far too exotic to be an ordinary, run-of-the-mill English businessman.

What did surprise her was the edge of accusation that threaded through his voice, and his use of the name she had discarded years ago as being utterly unsuitable to her image of herself.

'Salome Bouverie-Scott.'

It wasn't a query but a brief hint of a question did gleam in the depths of those black Spanish eyes and when she dipped her ash-blonde head in reluctant agreement the delicate skin on her fine cheekbones was stained pink with something close to embarrassment.

Perplexity followed as she watched his sensual mouth straighten with what looked like distaste because she hadn't used that name for years. Sally, the natural diminutive of the hatefully flamboyant Salome, had been discarded in late adolescence as sounding too slapdash, too frivolous. And as Sally was also the accepted diminutive of Sarah she had plumped for that, feeling it had far more authority, dropping the Bouverie part of her name because who needed it?

Somehow he had got hold of the names she had been blessed with at birth. But although it was puzzling it wasn't really important. Features serene again, she gestured once more to the vacant chair but his obdurate stance just inside the door didn't alter so she cast a brief glance at her wristwatch, bit back a sigh and asked calmly, 'How may I help you?'

Black eyes impaled her and his head was held arrogantly high above the impressive width of his shoulders, and there was something definitely intimidating about his penetrating, unwavering gaze.

It made her suddenly wish she'd asked Jenny to stay.

But that was plain ridiculous. Maybe his command of the English language wasn't so hot and he was searching for words. But time was passing. She would be late for her date. Nigel hated unpunctuality and, come to that, so did she.

Stifling the impulse to shoot another glance at her watch, she gave the stranger a cool, encouraging smile and he spoke then, the clipped words at strange variance with the throaty, almost hoarse dark velvet voice, as if he was trying hard to contain some kind of elemental, nameless emotion.

'You may help me by telling me where to find Piers Bouverie-Scott.' Strong, blue-shadowed jaw out-thrust, the sensual lower lip pugnacious, he regarded her down the length of his arrogantly aquiline nose, his hands planted on his non-existent hips now, parting the perfection of his tailored jacket to reveal a waistcoat that moulded his upper body with understated sartorial elegance.

Sarah's initial heated reaction was that he had wasted her precious time. Her second was to control her annoyance, rise fluidly to her feet, close the leather-bound diary and reach for her handbag, extracting the keys.

'I'm sorry, I can't help you there, Mr—Señor...?' She stopped, her cool smile cut off as an oblong of white pasteboard flipped through the air, landing on the polished surface of the desk. Not thinking, she picked it up. She had no interest in his name, but found her eyes skimming the black letters all the same. Francisco Garcia Casals. 'I have no idea where my father is, Señor Casals.'

When had she ever had more than a vague notion of where her remaining parent might be? Wherever he was, he was probably creating a ruckus and she'd eventually have the unenviable chore of reading all about it in the Press. The seamier tabloids always had a field day when Piers went on the rampage.

'My name means nothing?' He sounded as if he didn't belive her. 'Or Encarnación?'

'Should it do?'

Aquamarine eyes gathered a frown. He was still planted in front of the door, blocking the way. She wondered how many tons of dynamite it would take to shift him and then shuddered because he began to move towards her, long, lean legs narrowly clothed, slim hips barely moving at all. She thought, He walks like a matador, then swiftly told herself not to be so all-fired silly because she had never seen a matador in the whole of her twenty-eight years and for all she knew they might have to be transported in a wheelbarrow on account of wounds collected in painful places.

Then she heard herself gasp because, for one thing, it was utterly out of character for her to indulge in such juvenile flights of stupidity and, for another, he was looming over her now and for the first time in her adult life she had the strangest feeling that she wasn't in control of the situation.

'Then you would be wise to make it your business to find out because until I am satisfied my name and that of my sister will mean a very great deal to you.'

'I don't know what you're talking about.' Was that her voice? That thready whisper? And 'looming' wasn't the word. His proximity was swamping her, engulfing her in waves of confusion. Only because he was talking in riddles, she assured herself stoically. Why should his name mean anything to her—let alone his sister's—Encarnación?

The tip of her neat nose was on a level with his top waistcoat button. She took a rapid step backwards but sharp contact with the top of her desk reminded her that she didn't back down for anyone. She squared her shoulders and informed him sternly, 'Come to the point, Señor Casals, if there is one. I'm already running late.'

His wide shoulders moved in an eloquent shrug. 'All the more reason for you to tell me what I want to know. Tell me where your father is, and you're free to go.'

Her hackles rose with painful immediacy. He was talking as if she were his prisoner, as if she had no choices. Unease prickled her spine but she resolutely ignored it and answered precisely, 'You can't have heard me. I have no idea where Piers is at the moment. I had a card from him at Christmas and that was the last I heard. It was postmarked Edinburgh, but that's no help because he often makes a point of being in Scotland over Hogmanay.'

She didn't add that he liked the company of a certain Scottish widow who stroked his massive ego, fed all his voracious appetites and sent him lovingly on his way to pastures new a happy man. Annie Kelp had been an artist's model in her heyday, before her Junoesque figure had become richly rotund, and entertaining the great Piers Bouverie-

Scott took her back to the wild bohemian days of her young womanhood.

'He has no fixed abode?' The Spaniard made it sound like a crime and Sarah was almost in sympathy with him. Unfortunately—or fortunately, as Piers would have had it—there were plenty of Annie Kelps scattered around the globe, women who were only too happy to offer succour to the supremely talented, wildly rumbustious artist.

Piers never let a mistress go; he collected them— to Sarah's deep mortification—as other men might collect rare postage stamps and he loved the female sex far too much to let them go. Once they were hooked they were well and truly hooked. Sarah couldn't understand it. Didn't any of them know they were on a hiding to nothing, being used? Or didn't they care? Was each and every one of them happy to be taken advantage of provided she had the opportunity to enjoy the exhilaration of his company every now and then?

She sighed, shaking her head in answer to his question, then gathered her thoughts.

'Why do you want to find him?' It couldn't be money. Piers, for all his manifold faults, paid his bills. People fought to acquire his latest paintings. He could charge what he liked, and did. He probably had no idea how wealthy he was. His agent, Miles Hunter, handled all his financial affairs.

Nevertheless, Sarah knew instinctively that whatever it was this man wanted it wasn't to shake her father by the hand, congratulate him on his genius, beg him to take a commission. And, even though her wayward parent had been a source of continual and often excruciating embarrassment for as long as she could clearly remember, she would never disclose his whereabouts—even if she knew them—to anyone who might harm him.

'You are telling me you do not know, cannot make an educated guess?' Cynical disbelief stared out of his eyes. 'You cannot be unaware of your father's reputation. It is legendary.' His dignity at this moment was chilling and Sarah quickly averted her eyes.

She was certainly no stranger to her father's reputation. But it was something she tried to forget. His crazy nomadic lifestyle, the months of hard work when nobody knew where he had hidden himself away, followed by wild parties, his affairs—endless affairs—and his explosive temperament earned far more comments in the tabloids than his creative genius.

But surely her father couldn't have stolen this man's wife or lover? She couldn't imagine any female in her right mind preferring the older man, even if bombarded by the vital life force that seemed to trap most people who came into contact with him, over this undeniably spectacular specimen of Spanish manhood.

Realising she was fiddling with the office keys, tossing them from one hand to the other, she stopped herself at once. She never fidgeted, and certainly wasn't about to start now.

'Suppose you tell me,' she uttered coldly. 'I really don't have time to play guessing games.'

He gave her a look that was sheer enmity and his voice was raw with disgust as he told her, 'Your father seduced my sister. He has taken her away with him. Encarnación is barely eighteen years old. Her life was sheltered, protected, until that *demonio* spoiled her!' His black eyes blazed, his passionate mouth pulled back against his dazzlingly white teeth. His fury filled the room.

Sarah groped for the chair and sat down quickly. If what he claimed was true, then he had every right to be angry. But surely he had to be mistaken? Piers had dozens of affairs, some of which had been going on for years, but never, as far as she knew, with young inexperienced girls. His tastes ran to the more mature type, women who would mother him, smother him with love, asking for little in return except the glow of his reflected glory, basking in it for a little while until he roamed away again.

'Are you sure of your facts, Señor Casals?' She did her best to keep her voice perfectly level and incisive and heard the edge of anxiety creep in with alarm. One of them had to stay calm, and by the sizzling fury that came her way it wasn't going to be him.

He disdained to answer, extracting a folded sheet of paper from his breast pocket and slapping it down on the desk, glaring at her from hooded eyes as if daring her to argue.

Straightening her spine, she took the paper in cool white fingers. Its crumpled state told her it had been read and reread many times, but nothing more, although her father's name leapt from the page.

She didn't look at him. 'I don't read Spanish, *señor*, she said, and watched strongly lean olive-toned fingers snatch it back.

'*Por Dios!*' he growled, as if her lack had snapped what little patience he had. 'It says, and

I quote, "Do not try to find me. I have met someone who really cares about me. Where he is, I will go. His name is Piers Bouverie-Scott and that alone will tell you all you need to know."' He thrust the note back into his pocket, his skin tight with disgust. 'As your father's name is synonymous with wild orgies, reckless philandering and mistresses by the cartload, I am in no doubt as to what has happened to Encarnación. This note spells it out, if any further proof was needed.' His sensual mouth thinned ominously. 'When I find him, I will kill him!'

'Don't you think that's rather extreme?' Sarah said frigidly. She felt cold all over, through and through, but she recognised an uncontrolled temperament when she came up against it. She had had enough experience of handling Piers' volatile, creative personality in the past to know that the cold voice of reason was the only weapon. 'I'd like to help you,' she went on firmly, not letting him know how sick and cold she felt inside. 'But I truly don't know where he is.' She pulled the telephone towards her. 'However, his agent might.' Distasteful circumstances called for some sort of action.

'Miles Hunter? Do you think I haven't already contacted him—do you think I am *loco*?' He sent her a look of such heated derision that the hairs on the back of her neck stood on end. She wriggled uncomfortably in her chair as he pushed his extravagantly handsome face close to hers, his throaty voice bubbling over with scorn as he uttered, 'I don't sit around waiting for things to happen, I make them happen, *señorita*. I have made it my business to track down anyone who might know where *el diablo* is—his agent, the owner of the gallery where he habitually shows his new work, the people who supply his materials, all to no avail. Like the devil, he has disappeared in a puff of purple smoke...

'So finally I have come to you. You, the last slender hope. Few daughters would knowingly deliver a father into the hands of a man who was out for his blood. But one look at you, with your big icy eyes, gave me the hope that you were cold enough not to care! So by all means phone.' He pushed the receiver into her hands. 'Ask Hunter. He might tell you, where he wouldn't tell a stranger. Do it!' he ordered as she stared at him with shocked blue eyes.

Biting her lip, she dialled Miles Hunter's number, her fingers disgracefully unsteady. It was generally understood that first impressions were often the truest. Did this big, vital man really believe she was icy, cold enough to betray her nearest relative because she didn't have it in her to care?

It didn't matter what he thought, she told herself as she waited for her call to be answered, drumming the fingers of her right hand on the top of the desk. Her decision to call the agent, to try, in a small way, to help the Spaniard, had been instinctive. She was sure there had been a mistake, a crossing of wires. Reprobate though he was, Piers wouldn't set out to seduce an innocent young girl, and she could sympathise with Señor Casals' concern, his need to locate his run-away sister.

But that letter had been damning... Her arched brows knotted then eased again as Miles Hunter answered, and after a few pleasantries she asked, as coolly as she could, 'Do you know where I could contact Piers? I haven't heard from him since Christmas. Four months is a long time, even for him.' In her state of heightened awareness, she felt the Spaniard's black eyes boring into the back of her head, monitoring every word she said, and instinctively held the receiver closer to her ear. If, by a stroke of good fortune, Miles knew and divulged her father's whereabouts, she had no intention of allowing the looming, murderous brute to overhear it, get to him before she could.

'You're the second person to ask today,' Miles confessed, and she could hear the grin in his voice as he told her, 'This arrogant Spanish Don practically threatened me with the Inquisition. Obviously, I acted dumb. I don't know what your dear daddy's been up to this time—and don't really want to—but from the prolonged silence I'd hazard a guess that he's got his head down, working hard. In Spain, more than likely,'

'Well, I'm so sorry to have bothered you,' Sarah said, her voice coolly apologetic. 'If he does get in touch, let me know, would you, please?' Then she changed the subject, asking about his wife and family, allowing herself time to grab back her control.

She really should have made the connection herself. Encarnación was Spanish, her removal from her family home—wherever—obviously sudden. So it was highly unlikely that Piers would have met her in any other country but Spain. And therefore she knew exactly where to look!

When the spurt of elation had died down sufficiently she said her farewells and replaced the receiver, turning in her chair, her cool eyes fixed on a point beyond those intimidating shoulders, her voice clipped but not antagonistically so as she stated, 'As you've probably gathered, Miles doesn't have a clue either,' and mentally crossed her fingers, hoping he hadn't picked anything out from the agent's conversation. Expecting a renewed outburst of ferocity, she risked a direct look, but he was leaning against the filing cabinet, his arms crossed over his chest, and, far from snapping, the black eyes were almost slumbrous, their expression hidden by lowered olive-toned lids and sweepingly thick, lustrous black lashes.

Then, almost lazily, he levered himself upright and, with an almost imperceptible shrug, gave her, 'Then there is nothing left but to thank you for your time, *señorita*,' and sketched a bow of such courteous gravity that she was left speechless, staring at the space he had occupied for several long seconds after he had walked out of the office.

Somehow, strangely, she felt incomplete, as if his going had left something dangling, unresolved, oddly regretted. Which was, of course, she rebuked herself, utter nonsense. She had fully expected him to continue to harass and harangue her, had psyched herself up to deal with it—only to watch him capitulate gracefully, accept that she could tell him nothing, do no more. Which left all that adrenalin with nowhere to go.

And prodded her into immediate action.

She hadn't expected Francisco Garcia Casals to give up quite so easily. But as he had she took advantage of it thankfully, ignoring the irrational sense of disappointment. Checking that he had indeed left the premises, she sat at her desk, opened her personal directory and pulled the phone towards her.

Half an hour later she had booked her flight and cancelled her date with Nigel, who had, to her astonishment, turned quite nasty.

Their relationship of six months' standing was purely platonic as yet, although she had wondered, in her off-moments, if it could progress to something more, and permanent, because he was sober enough, conscientious enough to be that rare animal—a male she could possibly be persuaded to entrust her future contentment to.

But now she was quite sure he wasn't. If she ever allowed a man to become part of her life she certainly wouldn't expect him to throw a tantrum because, as she had explained, something urgent had cropped up, making the cancellation of their plans unavoidable.

Registering that she felt no regret at all, she contacted Jenny and asked her to take over the office for two or three days, phoned a local taxi firm because she didn't have time to waste on making her way home to her apartment—four rooms in a converted Victorian villa—by public transport, booked the same driver for the morning to take her to Gatwick and spent the evening packing and congratulating herself that by this time tomorrow she could well have cleared up the mystery of the missing Encarnación without ever having to clap eyes on the daunting Francisco Garcia Casals again.

CHAPTER TWO

SARAH, bouncing about in the back of the taxi, almost wished she'd given in to temptation and hired a car. The drive from the airport to Arcos de la Frontera was a long one and her ears were being assaulted by the raucous music coming from the radio, her nose by the aroma of cheap tobacco and a particularly violent brand of aftershave, and her eyes by the plethora of tawdry fluffy and glittery mascots bouncing around on lengths of coloured string.

But as she only intended to be in Spain for two days at the very most she had deemed the expense of hiring a car a luxury she could do without. No one could accuse her of being mean, but she had learned to be careful, not throwing her money around unnecessarily.

Awkwardly, she wriggled out of the severely styled dark grey blazer she had chosen to wear over paler grey linen trousers and a matching shirt Even in April the heat was astonishing. She had forgotten how fierce the sun could be in southern Spain and couldn't wait to get back to the cool English spring she had left behind. It was far more suited to her temperament, she decided tiredly, feeling an annoying crop of perspiration spring out on her upper lip.

Closing her eyes on the vibrant landscape, the terrifyingly twisty road, she picked over the situation that faced her.

On the one hand she could find her father alone, working like a man possessed, never having heard of the absconding Encarnación, in which case she would stay overnight and leave first thing in the morning with a huge sigh of relief.

Or—and this was the worst-case scenario, her secret fear—she could find him with his new young mistress and have the disagreeable task of making him see sense, pointing out, with graphic emphasis, what he could expect if Francisco Garcia Casals ever got within thrashing distance, trying to make the wayward young minx see the error of her ways and return to her family home.

That Piers would be at the house in Arcos, innocently or not so innocently, was in no real doubt now. When her mother had been alive they had often spent the spring there because Piers had always felt spiritually at home in the Andalusian mountains, executing some of his best work there.

After her death—when Sarah herself was only thirteen—Piers had closed the house up for a time but in later years he had often used it as a bolt-hole when he wanted to get down to serious, concentrated work.

He called it his *cabaña*, but it wasn't, of course. It was a small house in a tiny warren of streets in the old town, but, as he said, he liked the way the word *cabaña* rolled off the tongue. Her father, she thought resignedly, wasn't spectacularly clever when it came to seeing things as they really were.

And no matter how often she told herself that there had to be some mistake, the letter had been all too explicit. Impatiently, she dabbed her damp forehead with the back of her hand. It was all too tiresome to be borne and she could only pray that, as Encarnación had obviously met Piers at some time or other, the little minx had picked his name out of the ether and used it as a smokescreen for her own questionable activities.

The Spaniard had described his sister as being sheltered and protected—and that, of course, pointed to innocence. From the little Sarah knew of Señor Casals she guessed that translated into the fact that the eighteen-year-old had been utterly dominated by his sledge-hammer personality, that he expected his female relatives to stick to rigidly old-fashioned codes of behaviour, gave them no freedom whatsoever in a changing world, a world where female emancipation was the accepted thing in all levels of society, even here.

She didn't blame the unknown girl for wanting out of such a stultifying situation. But that didn't excuse Encarnación's abuse of Piers' name, if that was what had happened—and oh, how she prayed that it was. He was more than capable of making trouble for himself; he didn't need help in that direction from a Spanish teenager who wanted to toss a red herring or two in front of her big brother's aristocratic nose.

At last the driver flourished to an untidy halt, the ramshackle old Seat splayed across the narrow street, and Sarah scrambled out thankfully and paid him off, standing in the scorching sun for long moments after he'd reversed flamboyantly away in a cloud of exhaust fumes, trying to recover her poise after the hair-raising drive into the mountains.

Not many things gave her the jitters but bucketing around in the back of a car that had obviously long since passed its use-by date, driven by a man who took hairpin bends and horrifying gradients with as much apparent care as a swallow testing the thermals, was one of them.

Shuddering, she pulled herself together, becoming aware now of a round *señora* clad in voluminous black who was observing her with brightly inquisitive eyes from the doorstep of one of the neighbouring houses.

Alone in the tiny street, her father's house looked neglected and shabby. The others were brightly painted, the window-boxes and balconies brimming with abundantly flowering plants, whereas Piers' so-called *cabaña* had peeling paintwork, rusting balconies and seemed to sag, held up only by its neighbours.

But that was no surprise. When Patience had been alive she had done her utmost to keep up outward appearances, pretend that they were a normal family just like everyone else, creating a comfortable home wherever they happened to be— here in Spain in the fecund months of spring or in the rented stone cottage on a remote mountain-flank in Wales which had been the nearest thing to a settled home Sarah had had during her early childhood.

Her mother, she decided, not for the first time, had been aptly named.

Her father had never cared what his surroundings were like. He actually seemed to thrive
in an atmosphere of chaos and turmoil.

Bracing herself for the coming encounter with
her wayward, irresponsible parent, she pushed on
the bleached-wood door and found it securely
locked, then hammered without any real hope on
the grainy surface.

He would almost certainly be out in the surrounding countryside, sketching or painting. Why
hadn't she thought of that? She might have to wait
for hours before he decided to come back.

The watching woman shuffled off her doorstep,
bombarding her with a rapid carillon of Spanish,
and Sarah, who had long ago forgotten the few
words of the language she had picked up in her
childhood, smiled tightly, shrugging her slim
shoulders.

Her shirt was sticking to her in the heat. She was
getting a headache, felt almost sick with thirst and
almost had to add a threatened heart attack to her
list of unpleasant physical inconveniences when the
arrogantly confident, uncompromisingly masculine Francisco Garcia Casals said from directly
behind her, 'Having trouble, *señorita*?'

She twisted round, her insides clenching, her
heart palpitating wildly under her breasts. How in
the name of everything sacred had he got here?
Followed her? All the way from London? Determined to get to Piers and beat him to a pulp?

She couldn't ask because she couldn't breathe.
He filled all her space, stole the air from her lungs.
And he was talking to her father's neighbour, his
Spanish smooth and rich, a deceptively soothing

counterpoint to the elderly woman's shrill stacatto. Deceptive, because he turned and held her eyes with the penetrating blackness of his, telling her with a twisted sardonic little smile that curled her toes, 'Papá is away from home and not expected back for a number of weeks. But I have been reliably informed of his exact whereabouts.' His smile as he turned to his compatriot was warm and beguiling, making him look thoroughly gorgeous, and watching the way the woman bridled, a grin splitting her face, made Sarah feel ill.

They said all men were suckers for a pretty face but the same could be said for women. If a sexy man turned on the charm they went to mush.

Not this one, though. She had far more sense. Very aware of the problems her father could be facing, she fixed the wretched man with cool blue eyes and demanded, 'Then I insist you share the information.'

'Do you indeed?' One black brow drifted slowly upwards and she flinched under the impact of that slight, lopsided smile as he reminded her, 'Did you share your information with me? I think not, señorita. I suspected the agent had said something to turn the wheels of your cold little brain. You put me to the trouble of following you.'

He examined his square-cut, perfect fingernails briefly before shooting her a fiercely derisive look. 'I found the exercise highly tedious. Regard the withholding of my information as punishment. A just punishment, you must agree, when I tell you that the señora here described the "friend" who left with him. She was either my sister or her nonexistent twin.'

Hot temper glared in his eyes and, seared by it, by the damning information he had relayed, Sarah stepped back, her legs shaking.

And then he turned his back, the silky white fabric of his shirt falling in graceful folds from his wide shoulders, his mean and moody narrow hips and long black-clad legs moving with eloquent dismissive arrogance as he stalked away.

For a moment she simply stared. She couldn't believe this was actually happening, that he was walking away, refusing to tell her where Piers was, leaving her to stew in this heat, expecting her tamely to return to London, knowing that her headstrong, selfish parent had indeed seduced an innocent girl away from her deeply protective family, and wait for a call from a Spanish hospital to tell her that her father was hooked up to a life-support system in Intensive Care!

She gritted her teeth until they hurt. How could he do this to her? How dared he? He was not, she decided toughly, going to get away with it!

Grabbing her overnight bag and her jacket, she hared after his tall, receding figure, and was out of breath, her hair beginning to come down, falling all over the place, damp tendrils clinging to her temples, when she finally caught up with him.

And only just in time. He was already opening the door of an intimidating scarlet Ferrari. There was only one thing for it. Since she couldn't follow on foot she would have to prevent him leaving.

Using her last gasp of breath, she swooped over the cobbles and neatly inserted her body between him and the door, really hating him now for forcing her to behave like a hoyden, lose all her dignity, her highly valued poise.

He barely moved, only enough to accommodate her, and he didn't even look surprised. His conceit was monumental, his self-confidence appalling, she thought disgustedly, mentally grinding her teeth as she struggled to regain enough breath to make a few succinct demands.

But her breathlessness, if anything, was getting worse. And she was horribly aware of the hot metal burning her back as she was forced against the door by the infinitely more searing heat of his body. There was a strange tingling, burning sensation where her heaving breasts were thrusting against the heated male skin beneath that sinfully expensive shirt and she wasn't even going to think about what the pressure of those mean hips was doing to her abdomen ...

'Did you want something, *señorita*?' The voice was slow and rich and smooth, and was the slight glide and gyration of that hard pelvis really accidental?

Sarah gulped, her lungs fighting for air, and at that moment the rest of her hair fell down from its normal careful restraint, slithering in a silky blonde tumble to cloak her shoulders.

Her dazed eyes narrowed furiously; she hated feeling uncontrolled, hated him for making her feel this way, looking at her as if she were somehow amusing. Amusing! And much as she wanted to get as far away from him as physically possible she couldn't do it.

He knew where Piers was and intended to get to him and wreak his terrible vengeance. Even if he hadn't said as much the intent was there, deep in those black Spanish eyes. Come what may, she had to be there when the two men met up, to act as intermediary, a calming influence, at the very least.

He put his hands against the gleaming bodywork of the car, trapping her, the pressure of his hard, lean body increasing to dangerous proportions, and she shot out hoarsely, 'I demand to know——'

He cut in smoothly, 'Save your breath. I have no intention of telling you where *el diablo* is hiding, or of taking you with me when I go to take my sister away from his evil influences. It is a matter between him and me. You understand what I am saying?'

His white teeth gleamed dangerously and her stomach lurched. He meant it, he really meant it, and despite the years of embarrassment and annoyance, the times when she would have preferred not to have a father at all rather than one as wild as Piers, she knew she would do anything to save him from physical damage at the hands of this avenging devil. Her father, for all his faults and failings, she realised with momentary shock, meant far more to her than she had ever supposed.

Yet what could she do? He had already stepped back, removing the shatteringly unwelcome pressure of his body, his hands on her elbows as he shifted her dispassionately out of his way.

'Please, *señor*...' Her voice emerged as a disgraceful whimper but if she had to beg she would do it. Piers wasn't a young man and a violent encounter between him and this hard-jawed Spanish aristocrat with his damaged family pride and his lust for vengeance was beyond bearable thought.

'Please?' An eloquent black brow lifted in shaming derision. 'Don't try to appeal to my better nature. When my sister has been damaged, it doesn't exist. And you have no bargaining power. I have the information I need and you have nothing to offer that could tempt me to reveal it.'

That sexy accent growled through his voice and she stared at him with cold blue eyes. If he thought that lightly veiled insult would upset her he was making a huge mistake. She had no intention of making a bargain, certainly not the one he had conceitedly implied. There were some limits to what she would do to save her father's hide!

'However——' he dipped his head and the harsh sunlight gleamed on the dark luxuriance of his hair '—as I am not without honour, and you are a guest in my country, I will not abandon you in your obvious distress. Come.' He smiled grimly at her stupefaction, taking her baggage from her suddenly nerveless hands. 'I will take you to a hotel where you may refresh yourself, *señorita*. Where you may also hire a taxi to take you back to the airport. Try to find a driver who is a little less impulsive than the one you had before,' he added drily, opening the passenger door, stiffly formal now.

Formality suited her just fine. Much better than threats and insults, glimpses of a hot, wild temper, the way he had dominated her with his male body as if to impress upon her his vast superiority. Besides, she'd just had a wonderful idea. His reference to the driver who had brought her out had seeded it in her mind.

So she was feeling in control of the situation again as he manoeuvred the Ferrari out of the tiny colourful square, able to give grudging admiration as he negotiated the narrow streets in the shadow of the church of San Pedro, down to the lower reaches of the ancient town that straddled a towering rocky spur, finally parking in front of an imposing hotel, the potent scarlet car a shriek of affluence and power amid the humble waiting taxis.

She exited before he had time to come round to help her, pleased to note that her legs had stopped shaking, and her features were commendably serene as the Spaniard took her belongings in one hand and her elbow in the other and marched her up the broad, sweeping marble steps and into the foyer.

Her idea might not work, of course, for all kinds of reasons. But she would give it her best shot. And hopefully he would soon learn that he was not the only one who made things happen, took the prevailing circumstances and forced them to his will!

Inside, the foyer was all hushed, cool opulence, slow-moving brass-bladed fans overhead, marble slabs underfoot, intricate plasterwork and rich carved wood. And glass telephone booths, Sarah noted, filing the information tidily away, her stomach tightening with the excitement of knowing that her plan might possibly work.

'You are hungry?' her escort asked, apparently without a great deal of interest.

She shook her head without thinking. She was too wound up inside to think of eating now. But then she realised that if she had said she was ravenous it would have delayed his departure for a little longer, so she tacked on quickly, before he could walk away and leave her, 'I'd love a long cold drink, though, if you're having something,' and added,

'Might I freshen up first? Could you tell me where to go?'

'But of course.' He seemed bored now, and she tagged along as he approached the reception desk, but her spirits soared to fresh heights as he addressed the male clerk in English.

'The *señorita* wishes to use the rest-room. I shall be waiting in the terrace restaurant; will you bring her to me?'

Sarah barely registered the man's reply. It was all going better than she would ever have dared to hope. Veiling her aquamarine eyes in case they betrayed her mounting inner excitement, she extracted her shoulder-bag from the baggage he was still holding, said, 'See you in around ten minutes,' and headed smartly for the rest-room, ignoring his drawled 'Take your time', not caring an atom if he was regretting his decision to do her the courtesy of allowing her to refresh herself before he abandoned her to go off in murderous pursuit of her father.

He was going to regret his 'honourable' impulse far more before the day was out. She was about to make very sure of that.

CHAPTER THREE

THIS time round Sarah didn't in the least object to being jolted about in the back of a taxi. And she kept her eyes wide open. If they hadn't been screwed tightly shut for most of that earlier, stomach-twisting journey into Arcos then sooner or later she would have noticed the prowling Ferrari behind them. And been warned.

But, never one to take lingering backward looks at past mistakes, Sarah now kept her sparkling eyes firmly glued to the road ahead, on the unsuspecting speck of scarlet in the distance.

Little more than an hour ago, the gut-wrenching fear that Francisco Casals would roar off into the wild blue yonder, reclaim his erring sister then beat her father senseless, without her being around to stop it or temper the Spanish brute's ferocity, had seemed a frightening certainty. He had made her feel utterly impotent for the first time in years, and she hadn't liked the sensation one little bit.

But a few careless words of his had given her the idea of following him, as he had so obviously followed her all the way from London. And the rest had been amazingly, brilliantly easy. Even now, with her plan working out perfectly, she could hardly believe her good fortune, the way everything had neatly fallen into place without a single hitch.

A few seconds in the rest-room, just long enough to give him time to take himself off to the terrace restaurant, had been followed by a thoroughly satisfying whirlwind of activity.

The availability of public telephones had been a foregone conclusion and she'd been able to get through to her London office with hardly any delay, her tone brisk and concise as she'd told Jenny, 'Look, something's cropped up and I'm going to have to be away longer than I bargained for. Hold the fort for me, would you? I'll get back just as soon as I can.'

'Not to worry, boss. Take all the time you need.' Jenny sounded emphatic. 'It's ages since you had a break—just make sure you have a great time, and relax for just once in your life.'

Ordeal by a vengeful, tricky Spaniard was hardly her idea of a holiday, Sarah thought wryly as she replaced the receiver. But two could be tricky—as the lordly Francisco Garcia Casals would soon discover—and as for relaxing, well, there would be no time for that until she'd outwitted that black Andalusian devil...

Her shoulders straight, she marched purposefully over to Reception and asked the man she now knew spoke English—which had been another stroke of sheer good luck, hadn't it just?— 'Could you help me, please?'

'Sure.' He almost sprang to attention. 'Señor Casals is waiting on the terrace. If you'll follow me...'

His dark eyes showed no surprise at her obviously unrefreshed appearance but his brows did rise a fraction when she corrected him swiftly, 'In a moment. First, though, I need to arrange for a taxi—I speak no Spanish, I'm afraid.'

She ignored his openly surprised, momentary stare and followed coolly as he led the way outside to where three or four drivers were waiting for a fare, boredom or a kind of resignation written all over them. He probably couldn't understand why any woman would be thinking of transport when that suavely gorgeous hunk of Spanish manhood was waiting—especially a woman who must look as if she'd spent the last few hours fully dressed in a Turkish bath.

She didn't care what chauvinistic thoughts were rattling around inside his brain but embarrassment reared its debilitating head when he turned to her, bland-eyed now, asking, 'Tell me where you want to go, *señorita*, and I will translate.'

For one weak moment, Sarah was tempted to ask for the airport, to fly back to England and hide from the mess Piers had unwittingly got her into. But, she reminded herself, she had never run from anything yet, and wasn't going to start acting like a moral coward now. And she could weather a little embarrassment, couldn't she?

So she held her head high, looking down the length of her neat nose, toughing it out.

'I want a driver who is prepared to wait until Señor Casals and I leave. The *señor* will be driving the red car. I will want my driver to follow, at a discreet distance, naturally, to——' Her voice faltered, echoing the way she was cringing inside, but she overcame the slight problem and went on firmly, 'To wherever he goes. I am prepared to pay well over the odds.'

She refused to look away, even when he smirked with unconcealed amusement, just tilted her chin that little bit higher. She knew just what he was thinking. The handsome *señor*, who drove the kind of car only the seriously wealthy could afford to run, had grown bored with his English bit on the side—who could blame him?—and had dumped her. But the unglamorous, sadly plain creature wasn't prepared to be dumped, was determined to follow wherever he went, make a nuisance of herself. The conclusion was so obvious that she couldn't blame him for reaching it.

With a fatalistic shrug that implied that all men, even the mightiest, had to pay for their pleasures in the end, the receptionist spoke rapidly to one of the drivers and, the deal apparently clinched, turned back to Sarah, his smile very broad now.

'You wish now to join Señor Casals?'

'Of course.' It was difficult to maintain her dignity in the face of his amusement, but she managed it as he escorted her to the terrace restaurant. The incident would have enlivened his otherwise dreary working day. And if the sly, sideways glance he gave Francisco Casals as he rose to his feet when Sarah was led to his table was anything to go by they would both be the subject of endless jokes and speculation among the rest of the staff here.

Oddly enough it gave her a weird sense of fellow-feeling with Francisco as he dismissed the receptionist with a curt word of thanks. As if, in some strange way, they were bound together.

Which was complete and utter nonsense, she dismissed as she took her seat at the white-covered table, refusing anything from the lavish bowl of luscious-looking fruits, just accepting the glass of orange juice he poured from a jug that nestled in a bowl of crushed ice.

He was her father's enemy and that made him hers—because, whatever the rights or wrongs of the situation, violence was demeaning, it solved nothing, and she intended to be around to see that it didn't happen.

Ignoring the magnificent view of rumpled, sun-baked mountains spread out in front of the terrace restaurant, she gave him her full attention. There was a gleam in his eyes she didn't like—it gave her the mental shudders—so she ignored that too, offering him one last chance to redeem himself.

'You say my father's neighbour told you where he is, and that a girl answering Encarnación's description was with him when he left Arcos. And that you intend right now to go and find them.'

She took a sip of her juice to moisten her suddenly parched throat, horribly aware of the way his black eyes never once left her consciously prim features, and then a huge gulp of the cold, delicious liquid because that sip hadn't eased the annoying constriction in her throat. Then from somewhere she found the most businesslike tone she possessed and suggested sensibly, 'Tell me where they are and let me sort it out. I promise to separate them and personally deliver your sister to you. I sympathise with your concern, believe me, but violence won't solve anything.'

She couldn't put it plainer than that. It gave him the opportunity to rethink, to do the civilised thing and allow the whole unfortunate affair to be settled without aggression.

'No,' he responded unfeelingly, with not even a flicker of one dark eyelash to change his expression. He went on, his tone unaltered, 'Tell me, *señorita*, are you always so prim and pedantic, so completely lacking in passion? Your father is an undisputed amoral hedonist and he has seduced an innocent young girl away from her home, yet all you can do is say that you "sympathise with my concern"——' his mouth tightened dangerously, the fingers of one hand now tapping restlessly on the spotless linen that covered the table '—and mouth meaningless, bloodless platitudes about the ineffectuality of violence. Do you really think I'm the type of man who would be willing to sit tamely in the background and allow a woman to deal with my family problems? Do you think I have no pride?'

Something deep inside her shuddered. This man would never do anything tamely; a basic, atavistic intuition told her that much. No appeal to more civilised instincts, however sensibly couched, could reach him because, for him, civilisation was only a thin surface veneer. But only the restless fingers, the smouldering fires in the dark depths of his translucent black eyes told of the volcanic rage inside him as he continued in the same chillingly measured tone, 'If ever a man deserved a thrashing, it is your father. And I fully intend to teach him a lesson he will never forget. Without any interference from you. Now, *señorita*, if you have finished, I will find you a taxi to take you back to the airport.'

He got elegantly to his feet, his arrogant, remote features telling her more clearly than any words that she was dismissed, and, her eyes cloudy, she scrabbled around for her belongings, determinedly bottling up the unwelcome emotion that made her want to hurl her overnight bag at his head, wipe that superior, condescending expression from his face.

She straightened, quickly and nicely back in control again, firmly squashing that brief moment of insanity, her possessions held neatly in her hands. He had talked of passion and violence as if they were qualities to be admired. He disgusted her.

She had seen enough of both destructive emotions during her time with her father, witnessed the cheerful and, from her own viewpoint, utterly demeaning stoicism of her mother, and had made a solemn vow never to allow emotion of any kind to rule her life, mess it up and lead her into a state where she had no control over anything.

'That won't be necessary,' she told him coolly, her bluey-green eyes perfectly clear and steady now. 'The hotel receptionist has already dealt with it.' And she watched his tiny, elegant shrug, the small quirk of his beautiful, passionate mouth and put the sharp punch of sensation beneath her breastbone down to the sheer excitement of knowing she had outwitted him.

And now the sensation of churning, bubbling excitement was still with her, hardly containable. She had experienced nothing quite like it in the whole of her adult life. Ever since that proud chunk of Spanish manhood had assumed control—or so he, in his haughty arrogance, had believed—every

single thing had gone her way. Which meant that
the angels were on her side!

The red vehicle ahead disappeared from sight
round a bend on the twisty mountain road and she
was unconcerned enough to spare a glance at the
awe-inspiring scenery. Dry rocky ranges dropped
precipitously to deep river valleys mantled by the
green of olive groves and forest trees and somewhere here, in this remote and ferocious landscape,
her irresponsible father was hiding away with his
latest conquest.

But even her deep distaste for yet again having
to sort out the problems Piers had created for
himself was almost forgotten in the intense satisfaction to be had from beating the Spaniard at his
own game.

She had been eighteen years old when she had
finally decided that enough was enough, that it was
high time she abandoned her father to his own wild
devices and got on with her own life. She had stuck
rigidly to that earlier decision and going against it
didn't seem to matter now, not when they rounded
the bend and saw the Ferrari disappearing in a puff
of arrogant dust around the next.

Whatever his faults, Señor Casals was certainly
a careful driver. His sober speed couldn't have been
more granny-like if he'd set out to break a record.
Which begged the question of why he'd equipped
himself with such a potent piece of machinery in
the first place. The scarlet Ferrari was obviously a
status symbol only, a look-at-me macho statement
which he obviously had the financial wherewithal
to purchase but hadn't the bottle to use to its
powerful potential.

Smiling at her own inverted snobbery, she called a halt to her mental carping and gave hearty thanks instead for the way things were. If he'd put his foot down her driver wouldn't have had a hope in hell. The taxi would never have kept pace and she would never have been given the opportunity to walk in and temper the proceedings when the violent Spaniard met up with her culpable yet unsuspecting, unprepared parent.

But the impressive view that was now unfolding took her breath away, deflecting her thoughts. Great stone walling, fragmented in parts, marched down the precipitous mountainside, partly enclosing what she could see of a tiny village in the deep and distant, verdant valley below. And high above, straddling a rocky spur, dominating the craggy landscape from its austere, arid heights, the imposing walls, crenellations, turrets and towers of a massive castle soared to the raw blue sky.

As a statement of power and authority it would take some beating, she thought, then opened her eyes very wide as the scarlet Ferrari, with a definite flirt of its rear end, turned beneath an impressive archway that could lead nowhere else but to the castle itself.

Surely Piers and Encarnación weren't hiding up here? And apparently her driver had his own misgivings because he stood on the brakes, turning to her, gesturing expansively towards the archway.

'*Qué quieres, señorita*?'

She stared at him, wrinkling her brow. He was, she assumed, waiting for further instructions. Then she shook her head decisively. Discreetly following the vengefully violent Spaniard was one thing, sweeping up to the main entrance in a taxi was another. She couldn't afford to advertise her presence until she'd managed to slip inside. She didn't want every door bolted and barred in her face, to have to pace around outside, waiting while Señor Casals gave Piers the punishment he deserved.

'I'll walk the rest of the way,' she said firmly, then met his blank eyes. He didn't understand a word. Quickly she extracted her purse from her shoulder-bag and the driver smiled. That much he did understand and she paid him off, using most of her remaining pesetas, gathering her belongings and pacing forthrightly towards the arch and beneath it, not wanting to show the obviously curious taxi driver even the smallest hint of the panic that was beginning to beat its frenzied wings against the inside of her head.

Nothing to panic about, she assured herself, refusing to feel intimidated as the great stone arch swallowed her up. She'd been ultra-successful so far; now all she had to do was find a way inside the thick, looming walls and break up whatever mayhem might be going on inside. Put an end to it with the cool voice of reason. At the very least, Casals would surely temper his violence considerably when she appeared on the scene as a witness.

The idea that Piers might have brought his newest mistress to this isolated but obviously magnificently maintained place wasn't so unbelievable as she had first thought. His enormous talent, not to mention his larger-than-life personality, had earned him many friends all around the globe, some of them in distinctly exalted positions. She now had little doubt that the exalted personage who actually owned this overwhelming place had handed over the keys, no questions asked—and probably with the high-class equivalent of a nudge-nudge, wink-wink—so that the undisputed genius could enjoy his latest sordid peccadillo in splendid isolation.

The very idea made her stomach churn. She might be able to save Piers from a physical whipping at the Spaniard's hands but no way would he escape the scathing tongue-lashing she fully intended to deliver when she got him on his own.

Emerging from the arch, which, because the outer walls were so thick, had seemed more like a tunnel, Sarah took stock. It was early evening now, but the acreage of stone-paved courtyard was still bathed in sunlight. Even so, she slipped her arms into her jacket—the fewer things she carried the better—and carefully eyed the Ferrari which was crouched in front of what surely had to be the main entrance door.

She had the uncanny feeling of being watched but the massive building looked deserted—apart, that was, from the unoccupied scarlet symbol of machismo.

There was nothing to get goose bumps about, she assured herself. And, although the fortress-like structure might give an initial impression of keeping a stern and watchful eye on the tiny village which shimmered whitely in the heat haze down in the narrow valley, the martins nesting in crevices in the walls helped to create a delicate, swooping counterpoint and the stone of the castle itself was a lovely delicate honey tone, adding an air of almost fairy-tale fantasy.

Definitely not forbidding at all, she chided herself, then, as hovering in the shadow of the enormous archway making foolish assessments of the architectural atmosphere wasn't getting her anywhere, she squared her slender shoulders and set resolutely out across the massive courtyard.

She was here for a purpose and the sooner she got on with it the better. Once she'd taken a project on board she allowed nothing to deflect her from her purpose; that single-mindedness had helped make her agency the success it now was. Francisco Casals would soon find out that he wasn't dealing with an empty-headed female who was too feeble to stand up for herself!

The Spaniard had known exactly where to find her father, and even now the elderly man might be sampling a knuckle sandwich. Or worse. Her heartbeats quickened. She began to run. If the main door was locked it could take her quite some time to find a way in. And time was something she was short on.

She was dragging the warm dry air into her lungs in painful gulps by the time she reached the intricately carved stone arch that surrounded her objective—the main door.

It was thick and unyielding, studded and strapped with iron, and she twisted the great iron ring with misgivings, only to hear the infinitely satisfying click of the heavy latch, feel the great door swing inwards as if on oiled hinges. She barged straight through to the dim cool silence of the vast space beyond, adrenalin scudding through her veins, then stopped, disorientated, as the door closed silently behind her, making the dimness almost dark. And all she could hear was the rapid thud of her heartbeats. And the sound of someone breathing.

Her breath clogged painfully in her throat then emerged on a foolish squeak as that unmistakable dark, smoky voice said from directly behind her, 'What kept you?'

CHAPTER FOUR

Too shocked to speak, Sarah stood frozen as her emotions went into a state of riot, while her stunned, wide-eyed stare took in the glorious, olive-toned features that gave absolutely nothing away. That almost frightening inscrutability increased her whirling sense of dangerous disorientation. Then, thankfully, common sense gained ascendancy and she gathered her mind together. Fast.

His totally unexpected appearance had startled her, naturally enough, making her heart leap up into her throat with shock. But that moment was well and truly behind her and she could breathe a big sigh of relief, congratulate herself on achieving her aim.

Not stopping to wonder why he hadn't already begun his search of the huge premises for the missing Encarnación and the man he had vowed to beat to a pulp, she did nothing to hide the smile of sheer complacency that curved her soft lips as she suggested, 'We'll go and look for them together, shall we? And don't even think of asking me to wait outside until the shouting's over.' She gave him a glittering triumphant look from beneath her eyelashes. 'No one ever underestimates me twice in one lifetime, Señor Casals, so take my advice and don't try it again.'

Just to further impress on him that he didn't have the monopoly on tough-talking arrogance, she

44

straightened her mouth to a cool, firm line and glared haughtily down the length of her nose but his expression was still a total enigma and for some reason shook her all over again, because there was something behind it, a heavy, steely force that could confuse and frighten her if she didn't keep the upper hand.

And then a slow, beautiful smile spread over his face and that really worried her. She'd outwitted him, after all, so surely he had nothing to smile about! But she refused to step the few paces away from him that all her instincts were urging her to take because she didn't back down for anyone, certainly not for him.

'Together. Yes, I like the sound of that.' Genuine satisfaction honeyed the dark, smoky voice but the sudden trap of his fingers as they closed punishingly on her upper arm was a cruel contrast. 'Come, little fly. You walked into my web so prettily, and now we will wait. Together, as you said.'

Suddenly, the huge space seemed airless. Those dark, inscrutable eyes rested on her, seeming to map the way her brain was working as it tried to make sense of what he had said.

Wait? Surely he couldn't be saying that during the relatively short time he'd spent here ahead of her he'd had the opportunity to search the warren of rooms that must make up the interior of the castle? That he'd found someone—one of the staff maybe—who'd told him that Piers was out somewhere, that he'd turn up again if they waited?

It made no kind of sense at all.

She frowned, making a determined effort now to pull away, but that only made the punishing

pressure of his steely fingers more intense as he
began to urge her across the stone floor. She tried
to dig her heels in but it was impossible and she
had the horrible feeling that if she resisted further
he would pick her up and toss her over his shoulders
like a rag doll.

'Don't hustle me,' she snapped, doing her best
to sound fully in control and formidably stern. 'If
you'll show me where we're supposed to wait, I'll
go without being manhandled, thank you.' She injected a fine note of sarcasm but it made not a jot
of difference, except that she imagined she saw a
pitying smile flicker across his lips.

'And how do you know they're not in residence?' she persisted doggedly, doing her level best
to keep her breathing nice and regular, to ignore
the manacle of his strong, lean, inescapable hand.
'Dad's neighbour told you they were here but you
only arrived ten minutes before me, so you can't
possibly have had time to make a proper search,
and for all you know the owner might be here too,
and have us thrown out as mannerless intruders. I
don't suppose you've thought of that!'

She might have been talking to thin air for all
the response she got and by this time they had
emerged through another massive door, out of the
dim shadows and into the brilliance of an interior
courtyard, open to the deepening sun-shot early
evening sky. There were fountains, she noted agi-
tatedly, a single massive fig tree, masses of tubbed
exotic flowers and shady arcades surrounding what
she took to be the main living quarters.

Whoever owned this place was obviously a man
of considerable substance, not to mention clout.

But the relentless Spaniard hadn't taken her warnings on board. He had simply, and with insulting arrogance, ignored every word she had said.

Or so it seemed until he strode into the shade of the nearest pillared arcade and informed her, almost indifferently, 'I am the owner. And I can assure you that apart from a skeleton staff of two there is no one else in residence. Come, through here.'

Without giving her time to draw breath, let alone gather her thoughts coherently, he steered her through a deep archway into a cool, stone-walled apartment and up a narrow flight of twisting, banisterless stone stairs that clung to one of the inner walls. And her hair, hastily secured back in a makeshift knot with the few clips remaining following the slippery, silky descent in Arcos, flopped down all over again, obscuring her vision, and she could do nothing about it because the arm he wasn't clutching was hanging on to her bits and pieces. She felt hatred bubble up inside her, vicious and violent and quite unlike her.

The untrammelled mass of hair, tumbling to her shoulders and falling over her face, put her at a distinct physical and psychological disadvantage. She could barely see to put one foot in front of the other, was actually having to rely on that iron-hard hand to guide her. She loathed the sensation of having to rely on this over-privileged boor for anything and the conclusions she was beginning to draw did nothing at all to ease her state of mind.

At the head of the stairs he paused long enough to tell her, 'I phoned your father's agent from the hotel and gave him instructions to track Bouverie-Scott down and let him know that I would make an exchange. My sister for his daughter. Once contact is made I will tell him where he must bring her. In person. And then unfinished business may be conducted.'

His tone was conversational but that didn't take away the numbing shock of what he'd said. Sarah weakly allowed herself to be blindly led until he stopped before an ornately carved door and she squealed at him, 'That's kidnapping! You can't keep me here—it's illegal!'

'So arrest me,' he retorted drily. 'Through here, please, *señorita*.'

'Get lost!' she spat, kicking out frantically and trying to squirm away as he pushed open the door to what he obviously intended to be her prison for the duration. But he overcame her frenzied attempts to get away by placing both hands on either side of her slender waist and lifting her with contemptuous ease over the threshold.

As a prison cell the enormous, opulent bedroom came with a five-star-plus rating, she decided wildly. Medieval splendour successfully married with tasteful modern-day luxury. But that didn't make a scrap of difference. The principle was the same.

His hands slid from her waist and she rubbed her fingers down her sides, desperately trying to erase the raw, stinging sensation that his touch had left behind. She watched him shoulder the door back into its solid frame, saw him lean idly back against the carved panels as if negligently underlining her captivity, and dragged oxygen into her burning lungs.

'You phoned Miles from Arcos?' Her brows pleated. 'How could you be so sure I'd come here?

You said you knew where they were, but you refused point-blank—— Oh!' The shameful truth dawned at last and she felt a great tide of burning colour wash over her face. She felt such a fool, and hated it.

'Exactly,' he said drily. Then, his tone reeking of boredom, he admitted, 'I left out some of the truth when I translated what the helpful *señora* was happy to tell us. She keeps an eye on the house when your father is absent—it's an arrangement they have. He left a few days ago for an unspecified length of time and didn't say where he was going. But a young woman exactly answering Encarnación's description was with him.'

He held up an imperious hand when she opened her mouth to tell him exactly what she thought of liars, his sudden ferocious frown pushing the words back down her throat. 'I am a reader of souls, *señorita*. You have a cold, suspicious mind. Had I offered to drive you here on the pretext of confronting your wretched father with his sins, you would have immediately suspected my change of heart and removed yourself. My plans for your father don't involve having you running round loose, free to warn him.'

One dark brow shot up to his hairline. 'And you would warn him, help him avoid the justice he deserves—perhaps, even for you, blood is thicker than water. I couldn't take that chance.'

He shrugged minimally, the tiny dismissive gesture making Sarah's blood run cold. 'I decided that you were the best bargaining counter I had in my quest, and decided to help you to follow me. I allowed you to know how I'd kept track of you, just to sow the seeds of the idea. Made sure you knew which receptionist spoke your language, gave you ample time to make your arrangements——'

'How did you know I wouldn't see through it?' she blustered, furious with herself because he'd led her by the nose. She'd been too busy congratulating herself over outwitting him to notice the obvious 'help' he'd been giving her. And his drawled answer didn't raise her bruised self-esteem any higher.

'There was a risk,' he conceded, tacking on drily, 'But not a very large one. Your arrogance outweighs your intelligence, *señorita*. You set out to do something and you achieve it, coldly believing that no one will stand in your way. As I told you, I'm a reader of souls.'

Sarah's palms burned to hit him. How dared he make such snap judgements? He barely knew her, much less what made her tick. She would honestly have admitted to being single-minded, with clearcut views about the way she wanted to run her life. But arrogant? Never! And if she'd allowed him to make a fool of her then it was only because she'd been too worried over what might happen to Piers if that black-hearted monster got his hands on him.

'You can't keep me here against my will!' she reiterated shrilly. 'What do you take Miles Hunter for? A fool?' Her eyes blazed with blistering, nearly hysterical scorn. 'After getting such a threatening message concerning one of his clients, he will have already been in touch with the police—and they'll track you down and lock you up and throw away the key. Which is what criminal oafs like you deserve!'

'Not if he has any thought for your father, he won't.' He sounded almost bored again and thinly veiled impatience glinted in his black eyes as he added insultingly, 'Compose yourself, *señorita*. Try to find some self-discipline from somewhere. After all, I'm quite certain you believe you've cornered the market in that commodity. Treat this apartment as if it were your own. You may be here for some time, so you might as well settle in and get used to it.' He shot her a last, contemptuously dismissive glance. 'I'll be back when you've had time to control yourself.'

With that, he spun round on his heels and walked out, closing the heavy door quietly. Which was worse, she thought disjointedly, than if he'd slammed it. She heard the key turn in the lock and shuddered. Cold now, the heat of her panic and anger subsiding into a sick sense of inevitability, she wrapped her arms around her quivering body and squeezed her eyes tightly shut.

She would not cry. She would not!

And although Francisco Garcia Casals was obviously mad with damaged family pride, a throwback to the Inquisition, he had spoken the truth when he'd referred to her loss of control.

His mention of her lack of self-discipline— though who could wonder at it in the circumstances?—had struck right through all that uncharacteristic and fruitless rage. It was something she had to remedy, and quickly. Willing the shakes out of her limbs, she forced herself to take several deep, calming breaths.

Shrieking like a fishwife wasn't the way to subdue an enemy, she reminded herself tautly. That her

captor showed every indication of being utterly un-
subduable—by anyone—was something she wasn't
going to think about.

Barely sparing the opulent furnishings a glance,
she walked purposefully to one of the many
windows that marched down the length of the far
wall, dragging open the louvred shutters. The interior courtyard they'd entered by was far, far
below, the smooth, sun-warmed stone walls holding
no viable footholds whatsoever. She turned back
into the room, sighing disgustedly, and began to
wrench open the interior doors.

The first led to a beautifully appointed sitting-
room, which didn't interest her in the slightest, and
the second to a bathroom, which interested her a
lot. The third and final door opened on to a spiral
stone stair which would lead, at a guess, to the
battlements she'd seen from below. Closing the
door on that impossible escape route, she gave up
and marched into the bathroom.

Since he'd locked the only entrance to the suite
of rooms and she couldn't get out through the
windows or conveniently sprout wings and fly from
the battlements, she would have to try to cultivate
patience and forget any ideas of escape for the time
being.

She was almost completely sure that the wretched
man meant her no physical harm, personally, so
the only sensible thing to do was to try and reason
with him. And she herself would be in a calmer
state of mind, better able to persuade him that what
he was doing was madness, if she could at least
soak the stresses and stickiness of the day away in
a nice soothing bath.

And the surroundings could have been expressly designed with relaxation in mind, she decided, her mind freed now from the muddle of indecision and panic and sheer rage, enabling her to take stock for the first time since he'd manhandled her into the apartment.

Misty, silvery pale marble lined the walls, ceiling and floor and glass shelves floated ethereally, looking too insubstantial to bear the weight of the crystal bottles of perfumed bath oils, rare essences and costly body lotions. The partly sunken bath looked big enough to swim in and the wide surround was bedecked with graceful ferns in alabaster pots.

In a place this size the skeleton staff of two must have their work cut out maintaining such perfection, she thought as she turned on the dolphin-shaped gold-plated taps and watched the water gush steamily into the bath before gathering her thoughts and stripping thankfully out of her wrinkled clothes.

At least she wasn't alone here with the dauntingly unpredictable, fiery-tempered Spaniard, she thought as she added oils generously to the water. There would be someone around she could appeal to if he ever allowed his violent antipathy towards her father to spill over on to her. And she might be able to persuade one of them to help her get out of this place and back to civilisation and sanity. It wasn't totally beyond the bounds of possibility, she comforted herself.

The oils she had lavishly added filled the room with the sweet perfume of lavender, jasmine, rose too, she decided as she slid blissfully into the warm depths, and some other essence she couldn't quite put a name to. Whatever, they had obviously been blended with complete relaxation in mind because the stresses and worries of the long, troubled day seemed to melt away and, in the perfumed mists of the seductive fragrances, the hedonistic surroundings of the luxurious bathroom, the soft, silky warm water, even Francisco Casals became a force that could be reasoned with.

Sarah might have stayed exactly where she was all night, adding extra hot water and oils when she felt the impulse, but for the thought that she'd end up looking like a pale pink prune. So she eventually pulled herself languorously out, her toes curling into the thick-pile bath-mat as she released her hair from the heavy plait she'd secured on the top of her head with her one remaining hairpin and let it cascade down over her shoulders.

When she'd dressed she would sit down quietly—perhaps in the graceful sitting-room she'd poked her head into—and sensibly work out how best to reason with her unreasonable captor. Common sense and logic would be the best, the only way to get through to him, she decided, wrapping herself in one of the luxurious dark green towels before padding through to retrieve her overnight bag from the bedroom, relaxed enough now to mourn vaguely the fact that apart form a change of underwear and a nightie she had brought nothing with her.

It was dim in here now with velvety twilight but she would look for the light switches later because she could still see her way around and this soft bluey light was soothing. Reluctant to get into her travel-creased trousers and blouse when her skin felt so deliciously soft and fresh after her unaccustomedly long wallow, she hung her jacket in one of the capacious hanging cupboards she discovered behind a set of sliding doors. Reaching up, she lost her precarious grip on the towel, and she stepped over it where it pooled to the floor, enjoying the subtle caress of the cooler evening air on her body—then went into shock as the door opened and her dark captor walked in.

He must have depressed a light switch because every lamp in the room and the two delicate crystal chandeliers overhead glittered into immediate light. Shamefully revealing light, she realised as her insides twisted and tightened in panicky knots when she saw his black eyes slowly rake over her nakedness.

Ineffectively trying to cover herself with her hands, she made a raw sound in her throat as she stepped slowly backwards, trying to locate the fallen bath-towel with her feet. She didn't dare take her eyes off him.

He was holding her hostage, she had known that even before he had bundled her into this suite of rooms and locked her in, but this was the first time she'd felt afraid. Really, gut-wrenchingly afraid.

There was something elemental in those sensually raking black Spanish eyes, something that threw her body and mind into terrified confusion. Every minute hair on her body seemed to be standing on end, her skin burning, and to her horrified shame she felt her breasts harden, engorged with something new and nameless beneath the open caress of his eyes. Her body couldn't have responded more if he'd been physically touching her.

The tiny rattle of china and glass as he put the tray she'd scarcely registered he'd been holding down on a heavily carved table at the side of the door gave her the break she'd been looking for, and she twisted round, scooped up the towel and wrapped it around her trembling body, only to have the breath knocked out of her lungs, as if she'd been punched, at the mortifying sound of his slow, insolent hand-clap.

'Bravo!' One dark brow drifted slowly upwards and his sexy mouth curled sideways. 'I congratulate you on your act of startled modesty, but there is no need to stage it for my benefit. How long have you been wandering around naked, wondering when I'd return, as I said I would?'

He rocked back on his heels, his hands pushed negligently into the pockets of his beautifully tailored trousers, and the expression in the midnight eyes between the thick tangle of black lashes was derisive as he told her, his husky voice mocking, 'I would never have guessed it, but you have obviously inherited your father's over-active libido. But let me make it perfectly plain—you won't buy your freedom or my forgiveness for what he has done that easily, Miss Bouverie-Scott. However, you are welcome to continue to try.' He smiled wickedly. 'It wouldn't work, but it could amuse me, help to break the tedium of waiting.'

He turned then, opening the door. 'I will leave you to grapple with your frustration alone. And eat your supper; we don't want you losing weight, do we?'

And his insolently amused parting shot echoed in her head long after he'd locked the door behind him, boiling her brain with impotent fury, with the gross unfairness of his calculated insults.

'Who could have guessed that under the prim, unfeminine clothes you choose to wear an exquisite body exists, aching to be touched? Please feel free to display it for my enjoyment whenever you feel the urge.'

CHAPTER FIVE

SOMETHING dragged her up from the blissful oblivion of sleep. Sarah slowly opened her heavy eyes to the thick soft darkness and listened.

Still and utter silence.

She had probably been dreaming; that was why she had wakened, she rationalised drowsily.

She didn't want to be awake; she didn't want to find herself going over and over her unenviable situation again, her mind whirling round in circles. Neither did she want to remember her embarrassment, or the disgusting insults he'd thrown at her in that silky soft voice of his. No, she most definitely did not want to dredge all that up again. Not now, not until the morning, when, after a restful sleep, she would be able to think more clearly.

The fight for sleep had been a desperate one, her mind trawling through the facts as she knew them until she'd felt as if the inside of her head would burst into flames. That he'd made a complete fool of her had been hard enough to swallow, but his keeping her hostage was much, much worse, and as for the embarrassment, the insults, the way he believed she was trying to buy her freedom with her body... Words failed her...

And the new edginess, the fear, had kept slicing right through every other troubled thought, making her go cold with dread.

Even though she was as sure as she could be that she had no reason to be afraid, that he meant her no personal harm because she was merely the bait to pull Piers into this magnificent stone web, the irrational, unnameable fear kept coming, stalking her. It was as if Francisco Casals had pressed an invisible button and made it happen.

With an effort, she calmed her breathing right down and closed her eyes. She couldn't endure another battle for sleep and if she didn't rest both her body and mind she would be in no fit state to reason with the dreadful man in the morning.

The mattress dipped. The light bedcovers tweaked.

For an endless moment Sarah lay in icy shock. Something had woken her. Something had got into this bed with her! She could hear it breathing!

With a choking gasp of terror, she clawed her way to the edge of the bed. Her heart was going to burst. The back of her practical cotton nightie was grabbed by a lazy fist and the high-pitched squeal that vented from her lungs was overlaid by a relaxed, 'What do you think you're doing? Go back to sleep.'

It took her a few breathless seconds to banish all those nameless, night-time horrors and then she made another determined effort to leave the bed, hearing the rending of cotton as he refused to release her.

With a huff of outrage she scrabbled for the heavily carved bedside table, found the lamp and switched it on. At least this horror had a name. That smoky, sexy voice was unmistakable. And she could deal with him, of course she could. She would never allow herself to doubt that, not for a single moment.

As the soft light gilded the room, she twisted round, bouncing into a sitting position, giving him the benefit of her iciest stare. Then she looked away again. Quickly. All that smooth olive skin covering those hard, rangy shoulders, the power of that shatteringly masculine chest, the flat, lean stomach, the arrowing of crisp black body hair that disappeared beneath the fine white sheet... He appeared to be wearing nothing at all!

Her mouth went dry.

Had he no shame? No decency? Or was he confidently expecting her to try to buy her freedom? She remembered what he'd said about her inheriting her father's over-active libido and felt herself blush, right down to the soles of her feet. But although her voice was unsteady she managed to demand, 'Get out of this bed. Now!'

From the corner of her eye she saw him hoist himself up on one elbow but kept her gaze unwaveringly on the far side of the room, ready to leap to the floor if he so much as moved a single inch towards her.

But he didn't. He merely remarked with derisory patience, 'This is my suite of rooms, my bed. Why should I vacate it?'

'Because you put *me* here,' she answered thinly. She would have thought that was perfectly obvious.

'Naturally.' He twisted on to his back, his arms crossed behind his head, perfectly, obnoxiously at ease. 'You could be here for quite some time—it all depends on how quickly your father responds to my demands, how much he cares for you. So in

order to explain your presence to Rosalia and
Marcos I let them believe you were my woman.
Where else would I put my woman but in my bed?'

And that would make sense in the twisted, devious, wicked labyrinth that passed for his mind,
she decided furiously. She spat out, 'Then go and
sleep in the other room! There are some perfectly
comfortable-looking chairs and sofas, as I recall.'

'I do not sleep on chairs,' he said with the lofty
arrogance that made her want to slap him.

The need to give vent to her boiling emotions by
resorting to crude physical violence appalled her.
Sensible Sarah Scott brawling and sounding off was
not a picture that pleased her. This impossible man
had an unnerving habit of making her act out of
character, showing her a side of herself she hadn't
known existed and was certainly most unhappy
with.

Hastily gathering her split and ruined nightdress
around her rigidly outraged body, she slid smartly
off the bed, telling him tartly, 'Well, if you won't
I will.' She would have chosen to sleep on a clothes-
line rather than a bed that had him in it! And the
back of her neck prickled as she marched firmly
into the adjoining sitting-room, but he didn't say
a word, much less pounce on her and haul her back
to lie beside him as she had initially feared he would.

Closing the sitting-room door behind her, she
leaned wearily back against it for a second or two
before pushing herself into locating a light switch,
opening a couple of windows, selecting a sofa and
perching uneasily on the edge of it.

Her situation was impossible, and getting worse
by the second, she fretted, and she vehemently

wished she'd never set out to warn her father, advise him to send Encarnación back to her doting family or suffer the consequences of his own irresponsible, reprehensible behaviour.

She had always refused to believe in the old adage that whatever couldn't be cured must be endured. As her father had refused to be cured of his behavioural follies—and goodness only knew she had tried—she had, long ago, decided to endure it no longer and had gone her own way, leaving him to go to the devil in his.

So why had she decided to stick her oar into these muddled, troubled waters at this particular moment in time? she asked herself. A surfacing of filial affection which was stronger than she'd consciously known? An acknowledgement, at last, of her pride in his genius—a pride she had always tried to smother beneath clouds of disapproval of his wild lifestyle?

Whatever, soul-searching wasn't going to get her out of her present predicament, was it?

She arranged a cushion at one end of the sofa and curled up, trying to get comfortable. What she should have been concentrating on was the best approach to take when trying to reason her way out of the mess Piers had landed her in with that utterly impossible Spaniard.

Or not. She scowled into the cushion. What she really should be doing was emptying her mind of all contentious matter and getting some rest!

But it was easier said than done, and two hours later she was further from sleep than she'd ever been, fidgeting and wriggling and, worse, needing to visit the bathroom.

Which meant going through the bedroom, from which her black-hearted captor had effectively banished her, disrupting her sleep, taking over the big, blissfully comfortable bed, forcing her to find what rest she could on one of the sofas. Because surely he hadn't actually expected her to lie with him, their bodies barely inches apart—his naked as the day he was born and probably wallowing around during the night, tangling with hers?

The mind pictures that popped up into her head were alarming, adding another, deeper layer to her heated discomfort. She thrust them decisively away. She had quite enough to contend with without that!

Squirming to her feet, she assured herself that the oaf was certainly sound asleep by now. His conscience wouldn't keep him awake because he almost surely didn't have such a thing.

Tiptoeing to the door, she opened it a fraction and listened intently. No sound but his soft, regular breathing. Holding her breath, she padded silently through, moving slowly, making sure she didn't bump into furniture as she wended her way to the bathroom. And she stayed there as long as she dared, aware of the fact that he too might need to make a nocturnal visit.

That possibility was more than enough to have her creeping back out, reluctance to face another few hours of tossing and turning on the sofa making her pout. She hated the self-centred, arrogant brute for putting her through all this, she really did, and she racked her tired brain for a way to pay him back. She couldn't come up with a single thing. Except the resolve not to spend another minute stewing on that sofa.

Which didn't mean creeping back into that bed with him, of course. There had to be something else. And there was. Of course there was!

The third door!

It opened silently, like a dream, and the stair beyond was faintly illuminated by light-sensor bulbs set into the stone. Closing the door behind her, she padded on up, pulling open the stout door at the top and walking out on to the great rooftop, surrounded by the battlements.

The air up there was much fresher and cooler than it had been in the sitting-room, despite the windows she'd opened, and the pale fingers of dawn in the sky added to her unexpected sense of exhilaration.

Up here, at least, there was a sensation of freedom. Spurious maybe, but something she intended to hang on to for as long as she could because suddenly she felt much more alive than she could ever remember feeling before, could hardly wait for a new day to start, when she could begin again to pit her wits against the black-hearted Spaniard who, in her opinion, needed to be taken down a peg or two after the way he'd treated her.

Her eyes glinting with new-found energy, she fled over the huge stone roofing-slabs and leaned against the battlements, the stone rough beneath her hands, still holding a residue of the past day's warmth. She stretched over as far as she dared, squinting, eagerly trying to pierce the dark, velvety night for landmarks, and registered a sudden rush of bare feet a fraction of a second before she felt strong arms encircle her body, whirling her round to be crushed against a heaving, naked torso.

'*Idiota!*' His strong arms tightened convulsively as he dragged her away from the parapet and she could hear the rapid thundering of his heartbeats, feel the pulsating heat of his tall, sinewy body as her lightly clad flesh was crushed against him. 'Launching yourself down into a rocky chasm isn't the answer! I mean you no harm, you must understand that,' he assured her thickly, one hand sliding up to cradle her head, pulling it against the proud angle of his shoulder, his long fingers tangling in her hair. 'My quarrel isn't with you—you know that.'

The warmth of that smooth olive skin stretched tautly over hard muscle and bone was distinctly distracting, tugging her mind away from the obvious advantage he was unknowingly offering her. The intimacy of being held by him like this was clouding her senses, and when she felt the tremors of his inner tension shake his impressive male frame she had to fight hard to resist the impulse to cuddle in closer and surrender to the rapidly gathering sensations that were as strangely exciting as they were hitherto unknown.

Sarah shook her head desperately and fought instead to catch hold of the ideas that were poking at the edges of her fuddled brain, and he mistook the gesture, telling her rawly, 'If I frightened you, I'm truly sorry. And I promise you I will never lay a finger on you in anger. You will not be harmed in any way while you are a guest beneath my roof— consider your time here as a holiday. Will you do that, Salome?'

She could almost have capitulated to the urgency of his pleas, the very real—though utterly misguided—anxiety he had felt on her behalf. She had been on the point of coming clean, responding honestly to his deep concern, reassuring him that she simply wasn't the type to fling herself from a great height on to rocks, or whatever, no matter what dire circumstances she found herself in, because she had a whole heap more character than that, but his use of that ridiculously flamboyant name, the name she had firmly discarded years ago and which he had, in his meddling, prying, sneaky manner, somehow dug out, put her firmly on her feet again, back in control and knowing exactly how she would play this scene, get every last ounce of advantage out of the situation he had so conveniently misread.

The trembling part wasn't difficult because shock had ensured that she'd been shaking inside right from the moment when he'd crushed her into his arms, tugging her into the warm, safe haven of his strong body, but she had a hard time keeping her glee hidden, the exquisite pleasure of knowing that she could now get the upper hand and, hopefully, keep it, as she injected a weak quaver into her voice and said words she would never have believed herself capable of uttering.

'Why did you stop me? I—I can't bear it, I tell you! Locked away here with—with a violent stranger.' Her voice quivered nicely up to the level of hysteria as she tried feebly and ineffectually to pull away from him. 'You'd kill my father as soon as look at him—you said so yourself! What's to stop you killing me too? You'd have to, wouldn't you? To stop me from talking!' Her voice fell piteously. 'I can't stand it—waiting for the worst to happen. I'd rather—rather do—do anything. Anything at all! And——' she made herself give a huge gulp '—I can't bear being locked in. Not anywhere. It's enough to send anyone crazy!'

'*Dios!*' His voice throbbed with stress. She had made him feel a heel, guilty and ashamed of himself. Which was precisely what she had intended, ever since she'd realised he'd got her motives for being up here all twisted in his head!

That he must have a shred of decency in him somewhere, or he would never have felt the remotest pang of anxiety on her behalf, wasn't going to cut any ice with her because surely he richly deserved all the guilt she could manage to heap on his arrogant, much too handsome head, she decided very firmly as she closed her ears to his soft words of earnest reassurance.

But she couldn't ignore the way he swept her up into his arms and strode over the roof to the head of the stairway. How could she when he was cradling her close to that superbly made body? Especially as he wasn't wearing a stitch and every movement he made sent something that was a terrifying mix of fear and excitement scudding through her flesh, permeating her bones, weakening her. Moreover, if she breathed at all she could almost taste the elusive male muskiness of him, and she wasn't acting at all when she told him, panicking, 'Put me down. Please! I'm not an invalid. I can walk, you know!'

'Yes, I do know.' He held her even more tightly, if that were possible, as he descended the stairs; a furtively assessing upward glance revealed his set and sober features, the bones taut beneath the skin, and she quickly forgot to panic because she had just proved that she could handle him perfectly and rapidly suppressed a smile of total satisfaction.

She had got him worried, really worried, and, hopefully, very ashamed of himself. And that was just fine by her because he deserved every bit of sobering anxiety coming in his direction after the high-handed, careless, not to mention thoroughly insulting way he had mistreated and manipulated her!

So she would continue in her act as a near-hysterical neurotic with the tendencies of a lemming just for the immense satisfaction of seeing him grovel, make a fool of himself as he had tried to make a fool of her when he had dismissed her body with a look in his eyes that had said, Offer away, only I don't want it.

For that insult alone she would make him pay! And the day would soon dawn when he'd be un-locking doors, begging her to go, happy to release his hostage because he couldn't stand the guilt, would keep wondering when she would be driven to leap from the battlements again, or strangle herself with the bedsheets! His nerves would never be able to stand it!

She hoped she would give him a deep-rooted, life-long guilt complex.

Descending to the bedroom, he closed the door to the stairway with his foot and carried her over to the bed, settling her gently back against the pillows, brushing her hair back out of her eyes with a tender sweep of his hand. The prickle of searing heat from the touch of his skin against hers made her flinch and he sucked in his sensual lower lip and murmured deeply, 'Relax. I'm not going to hurt you. I don't break promises.'

She hadn't imagined he was about to. Somehow, she had always known he wouldn't do anything to cause her physical harm. The fear she had started to feel came from another direction entirely. She wasn't sure yet which direction that actually was. It was enough for now that his slightest touch did strange and unwelcome things to her.

But she wasn't about to enlighten him; she wasn't that much of a fool. Besides, she had her act to consider. So she gave a wobbly sigh, feebly closed her eyes and, after a long moment fraught with something that felt like deep consideration, sensed him move away. She risked a glance between her fluttering lashes.

He was pulling a pair of pyjama bottoms from a drawer in an antique chest and she swiftly closed her eyes again. The sight of all that virile manly nakedness was decidedly unsettling.

Tense moments later her heart jumped up into her throat as she felt the mattress dip and she opened her eyes in a wild tangle of lashes, her worst suspicions allayed because he was merely sitting beside her, marginally decent in pyjama bottoms that rode a little too low for her liking on his spare, lean hips. But that was better than before. Before...

'Drink this.' He was holding a generously curved crystal glass and she looked doubtfully at the amber liquid and hauled the bedsheet right up to her chin. 'Brandy, purely for medicinal purposes,' he added smoothly. He held the glass to her lips but she clamped her jaws together. He could feel as guilty as he liked because that, as far as she was concerned, was a wonderful bonus, but she refused to have him ministering to her.

He sighed, black eyes probing her wide aquamarine stare as if he was trying to solve some knotty problem or other, a tiny frown drawing the dark wings of his brows together. And then a flicker of amusement softened the sexy corners of his mouth and he practically purred, 'You didn't touch the meal I brought earlier.' He shook his head regretfully, one midnight lock of hair tumbling appealingly over his eyes. 'You were too frightened, too anxious?' he suggested sympathetically, and she nodded, laughing inside because he was picking up all the right ideas, letting him think what it suited her to have him believe when in reality she'd been too darned incensed to swallow anything.

Though, in hindsight, if she'd gulped down that bottle of wine she would, at least, have been able to sleep. But if she'd been snoring away in a drunken stupor she wouldn't have gone up on the roof and been able to take his mistaken apprehensions and use them to her own very distinct advantage.

'There's no need for you to be either,' he went on cajolingly. 'And your blood sugar must be low. So drink this up like a good girl. It will do you good, relax you, help you to sleep.'

The sleep bit sounded good to her, so good. It had been a long, tiring, traumatic day and waves of exhaustion were sweeping darkly over her.

She heaved herself into a sitting position, too tired now to bother about keeping the sheet firmly tucked beneath her chin, and grasped the glass he was offering with fingers that were numb with fatigue.

No worries, she thought as she sipped at the fiery liquid, hoping it would deaden her over-active brain and allow her body the rest it craved. Not a single one, now she came to think of it. Thanks to that episode on the roof and her own subsequent acting—playing the part of a feeble female possessed of a character as weak as water—his sense of shame and guilt would have him unlocking doors in the morning, driving her back to the airport himself and, in all likelihood, forgetting his threat to pound her father into the ground.

It was truly wonderful the way things had worked out, she congratulated herself as she gave him back the empty glass and settled herself comfortably into the bed, sighing with sheer pleasure because the best bit, the bit she liked most, was the fact that she had him in the palm of her hand now. He'd been completely, utterly fooled by her quick thinking, the way she had taken advantage of the situation that had presented itself!

But her wits made a protesting leap when he joined her, sliding beneath the sheets and flicking out the light, his big male body only an inch away from hers. And before she could give voice to a strangled protest he twisted over on his side, cuddling her into the curve of his body, murmuring softly, 'Sleep now, poor little baby. There's no need to be frightened, is there? See how safely I hold you?' As if to emphasise that particular point, the arm that was holding her tightened, the palm of his hand curving against her tummy.

'You don't need to hold me,' she managed thickly, physically having to force the objection out through the heavy tide of melting sensation that had its enervating source directly beneath his hand. And she wished, how she wished, she hadn't swallowed all that brandy so quickly. That, coupled with her mental and physical exhaustion, was making it impossible for her to find the resources to get herself smartly out of here and back into the adjoining sitting-room.

His long legs tucked more closely in behind hers as he contradicted smoothly, 'I have every need. I can't risk you running up to the roof and leaping out into the void again, can I?' He wriggled a little, as if thoroughly enjoying the feel of her neatly rounded bottom pressed up, as it unavoidably was, against his—well, she wouldn't let herself think of that.

She suggested on a highly suspect gasp, 'You could lock the door to the stairs and hide the key. That way you wouldn't have to worry!'

'Now how could I do that,' he questioned softly, 'when you have so graphically told me how the very thought of being locked in anywhere gives you hysterics? There will be no more locks to keep you in, only my arms to hold you, my body close to yours to give you all the reassurance you need.'

Reassurance? She had her doubts about that, she thought hazily, fighting now to stay wide awake and fully alert as his breathing settled down to a drowsy rhythm.

He had got her where he had intended her to be all along: cuddled up beside him in this sinfully luxurious bed.

But his reasons weren't the same as they had undoubtedly been before. No, of course they weren't. Then he had big-headedly expected her to buy her freedom with her body. Now his motives were entirely different, weren't they?

Of course they were, she reminded herself very quickly.

He was simply making doubly sure that his weak-minded, hysterical captive would not make a second attempt to do away with herself. He wouldn't want that type of scandal. It would bring dishonour on his no doubt illustrious and proud name.

On that reassuring piece of deduction she relaxed into the sheltering curve of his body and fell instantly and blissfully asleep.

CHAPTER SIX

THE rattle of china and the aroma of freshly brewed coffee woke her.

Sarah blinked her eyes rapidly and opened them to the warm golden sunlight which made the faded gold silk of the wall-coverings glow and shimmer, reflecting their light up on to the magnificent wooden mudéjar ceiling, and then her gaze homed in on the equally magnificent Spaniard.

At least he was up and dressed, she thought thankfully, surreptitiously wriggling further down in the bed for the sake of modesty. And that was a decided comfort, not to mention a huge relief, because she could have woken and found herself still held tightly in his arms, his warm male body curved protectively around hers, his hands all over the place.

Although, she had to admit uncomfortably, the very sight of him, so tall, so commanding, his hard, handsome face freshly shaved, his superb body clothed in leg-clipping black trousers and a flowing white shirt, set off a decidedly unfortunate chain reaction within her.

A reaction she simply had to ignore, she informed herself strictly. If you ignored something long enough it would cease to trouble you. Wouldn't it?

Her body had no right to respond so—so dramatically to this dreadful, lawless man. Her mind would take charge and dictate otherwise, she consoled herself. And she would dwell exclusively on the advantage she'd gained late last night. Work on it, make it come right for her. Because at the moment the down-side of the coin was his seemingly chivalrous need to give her his 'protection' in bed!

She had to make sure there wouldn't be a repeat performance, and——

'Do you always take this long to come awake?'

The dark, smoky voice cut through her mental ramblings and she looked at him from wary eyes, making rapid assessments. He had pulled a heavily carved, straight-backed chair to the foot of the bed and was just sitting there now, watching her between his thick lashes, the enigmatic expression he seemed to have mastered so well firmly in place.

She hated it when he looked at her like that. She didn't know what was going on inside that well-shaped skull. Was he about to fling open doors and let her go? Drive her to the airport to make sure she got on a flight back to England? Surely, after last night's performance, he wouldn't want the responsibility of keeping her here?

'What's the point in waking up to a prison?' she asked with thin petulance, just to ram her feebleness home—in the unlikely event of any forgetfulness on his part. 'You don't know how badly all this is affecting me.'

'Oh, I'm sure I do,' he replied with a silkiness that had her frowning. 'And your "prison", as you call it, is something we have to discuss. So drink your coffee and get dressed. We'll have breakfast together in the courtyard and talk it through.'

The smile he gave her was utterly disarming, as no doubt it was calculated to be, she decided cynically, ignoring it, locating the source of the heavenly aroma as she turned her head to the side-table where he had obviously placed the wide-bowled cup of steaming coffee as she had struggled up from sleep.

Breakfast in the courtyard, and a discussion, sounded hopeful. At least he was no longer planning on keeping her locked in here for the duration. If she handled the discussion part of it carefully she could be out of here and on her way by noon.

'If you insist.' She made herself sound uninterested. She reached for the cup. 'I'll join you as soon as I'm ready. I can find my own way.'

'I wouldn't hear of it.' Black eyes glimmered. 'After the fright you gave me last night I can't have you wandering around on your own. Who knows what you might take it into your head to do?'

Pig! He couldn't really believe, could he, that she was that unbalanced? Although he had been satisfyingly convinced by her charade last night. She was, she recognised crossly, hoist with her own petard. Smothering a sigh, she said demurely, 'Then you must give me the privacy to get washed and dressed in the bathroom.' With the door firmly locked, she added silently. But he gave her back a sorrowful shake of his head.

'Afraid not. You might hack your head off with one of my razors. Believe me, I'm no voyeur. But unfortunately you leave me no choice.'

She eyed him suspiciously over the rim of her cup, considering her options.

He looked sincere enough, but then she wouldn't trust him with an orphan's piggy-bank, let alone trust him to be up front with his enemy's daughter, the woman he was openly using as bait. Goodness only knew what was going on behind those black Spanish eyes. Concern for her well-being, after that splendid piece of acting on her part? Or something nasty and utterly, utterly devious?

As far as she was concerned, she had two options: refuse point-blank to move out of this bed until he had taken himself off, and risk making him too angry even to think about discussing anything, or allow him to think he'd won this round, meekly do as she'd been told and so be able to have that vital conversation while he was still in a reasonable mood.

Grinding her teeth with exasperation, she slid out of bed, grabbed her fresh underwear from her travel bag, yesterday's clothes from the wardrobe, refusing to look at him, and stamped into the bathroom, trying with one frantic hand to prevent the ripped nightie from gaping too revealingly.

He padded closely behind her, pushing the bathroom door back into its frame and standing in front of it, and she twisted round, quelling the instinct to yell at him, and managed to demand in clear, cool tones, her dignity commendably in place despite the strain he was putting on it, 'Do the gentlemanly thing and turn your back. I promise not to go near your razors.' Which was a touch tart, she realised belatedly, for someone who only hours ago had been supposedly rendered desperate enough to consider suicide as an option!

A flicker of what looked like amusement kindled deep in those fascinating eyes. But she couldn't be sure because he obligingly turned away. After giving his averted profile a quick hard look, she regretfully ruled both the bath and the shower out of play and made for the basin. She would clean her teeth, quickly wash her face then scamper into her clothes and earn herself a civilised discussion, one which would go all her way—provided she continued to play her cards right.

Her scanty ablutions over, she dragged her nightie over her head, moaning inwardly as she heard the fragile fabric rip even further, and as she emerged from the folds she looked up to find his innocently bland face directly in front of her. And slapped it.

He didn't even flinch. Just caught both her hands between one of his, holding her at arm's length. He looked, she thought wildly, as if he'd been used to women slapping his face every day of the week. And that made no sense at all because no woman in her right mind would want to slap this handsome devil. Except this one, of course, she reminded herself, tugging, trying to release her hands, feeling her face go crimson with embarrassment. But he simply held them tighter, his mouth curling softly, his velvet-soft voice shiveringly sensual as he asked her unforgivably, 'Why the virginal reaction? I've seen it all before, remember? You showed me.'

'I did no such thing!' she spluttered, outraged, but she might just as well have held her tongue because he went on, the light in the incandescent depths of his eyes kindling alarmingly, 'Seen every delectable inch, and held it all, cuddled up against me, me and those edible curves sinking together into a feathery mattress——'

'Just shut up, will you?' If her hands had been free she would have clamped them over her ears to block out that hatefully sensual voice. The things he was saying were sending her into a state of frantic confusion, and the way he was looking at her, his heavy-lidded eyes wandering lazily all over her body, had set up a heated internal quivering that was relentlessly taking her over. 'And let go of me!' she squawked through the breath that was sobbing in her lungs. 'I asked you to turn your back!'

'So you did,' he answered blandly, and she wondered hectically how he could look so innocent and yet be so wicked. 'And I did. But you didn't tell me for how long.' A twist of his hands diminished the distance between them to nothing.

Sarah groaned feebly as the pale globes of her breasts came into burning contact with the soft white fabric that covered his chest. Their shameful hardness would seem like an open invitation and her legs had gone, and any moment now she would have to cling on to him for support. And then where would she be? Back in that bed before she could say 'chastity belt'!

'Time to get dressed.' He took her by surprise; getting dressed was the last thing she'd expected him to want her to do. 'Or Rosalia will wonder what's keeping us from breakfast. Though she will probably make an educated guess, given the information I fed her.'

The cool slice of his voice cut through the hot muddle that had once been her mind and, disorientated, she felt him release her and only grabbed herself together when she realised he was holding her fresh lacy bra in one hand, the matching panties in the other.

'Give those to me!' She held out an imperious hand, desperately trying to tough it out, red flags of rage and deep humiliation flying on her face. Her eyes flashed blue fire. God, how she hated him! He embarrassed and humiliated her at every turn and when she thought of how he made her feel when he allowed his eyes to wander so explicitly over every inch of her nakedness she wanted to crawl into a deep dark hole and hide.

He advanced. Two languid paces. Her heart was pounding so fast and heavily that she was sure it was about to burst out of her body. His lean, beautifully crafted hands were still holding the lacy scraps and he said, with a honeyed smoothness that aggravated her beyond endurance, 'Now don't get so agitated. It's bad for your nerves. I'll help you dress and then we'll have breakfast. Won't that be nice?'

Nice! Nothing about the brute was nice! He was wicked, wicked! Dress her indeed! Did he think she was incapable? Stupid?

She twisted out of his path like an eel and made a dive for her clothes. Underwear she could do without. She rammed herself into yesterday's crumpled and travel-stained trousers and shirt, fastening buttons with frantic fingers, glaring up at him at the end of the undignified scramble, her gleaming blonde hair all over the place.

'There! Convinced I can get dressed all by myself now?' Her full lower lip jutted pugnaciously and she pushed her hair off her face with the back of her hand, wishing she hadn't lost all the pins, and saw him dip his head to one side consideringly as he moved towards her, dropping her undies on a stool as he came.

She backed in a panicky hurry, only realising when it was too late to do anything about it that she was against one of the walls, her retreat to the bedroom cut off by his predatory body. And then he was right on top of her, the hard thrust of his lean hips pinning her to the cool marble wall, his upper body angled slightly away as his long fingers lifted to the high neckline of her shirt.

'Leave me alone!' She tried to slap his hands away but he was too quick for her, too tricky, and the gilded patience in his voice made her grit her teeth with unadulterated exasperation.

'You've fastened the buttons all wrongly.' Warm fingers brushed the quivering hollow at the base of her throat. 'Allow me to straighten you out.' Gentle fingers, for all their steely strength, grazed down between her suddenly aching breasts as he released buttons, refastened them, his black eyes lowered intently to his task, those fingers moving, stroking, caressing, making her body betray her, putting her mind on hold, totally incapable of issuing the clipped instructions which would tell her how to combat this sensation of drowning in warm liquid honey...

'There. All done.' His eyes gleamed warmly into hers. 'You looked like a bag lady.' He ran his hand down the front of her shirt, almost impersonally, as if to satisfy himself that she was indeed tidier than before. but for Sarah there was nothing impersonal about it. The touch of his hands, the thrust of his hips against hers were threatening to send her spinning off into orbit. She hated herself for that mindless response but for once in her life couldn't imagine how to deal with the problem.

She almost sobbed with relief when he stepped back and took her arm, leading her out through the bedroom, telling her, 'Time for breakfast, unless you intend to spend half an hour fixing your face.'

She shook her head, too disturbed by what had happened back there to speak. She was grateful for his support as he led her back the way they had come yesterday, refusing to let herself care that he thought her face needed thirty minutes of fixing before it could be remotely fit to be seen, that in his opinion she looked like a bag lady.

It really couldn't matter less what he thought of her. But when he asked conversationally, 'Do you always dress in things that look like Chairman Mao's cast-offs?' her temper, gratifyingly spiked with righteous indignation, came fizzing back to her rescue.

She shook his hand away from her elbow, and her voice was good and controlled and decidedly icy as she countered, 'And whose fault is that? These are the clothes I chose to travel in. Comfortable and practical. It was not my intention to go haring over half of Spain in the blistering heat, or to stay longer than one night. Had I known I would be kidnapped and forced to stay for the duration I would have packed accordingly. Not,' she ended witheringly, 'that the clothes I choose to wear, or the way I look, has anything whatsoever to do with you.'

'Oh, but it does,' he responded equably, those fathomless black eyes appraising her slowly. 'When I shall have to look at you for an unspecified length of time, it becomes my business, I think. Don't you agree?'

She didn't. She most definitely didn't. But she wasn't going to bother to tell him so. Why waste her breath? She stalked ahead, down the length of the arcaded terrace to where she could see a table laid for breakfast on the far side where the morning sun angled in.

His opinion of the way she looked didn't hurt her; of course it didn't, she assured herself sharply. She was feeling all wound up inside and deeply miserable because of his passing reference to 'an unspecified length of time'. Which meant that although the events of last night had worried him, forcing him to keep watch over her at all times, he wasn't concerned enough about her mental and physical well-being to put her on the first flight back to England and rid himself of the responsibility.

But that was only a set-back. She would simply have to work at it, push home the advantage she'd so unexpectedly gained last night. Starting right now.

So she gave him a wan, die-away look as he lowered himself into the chair opposite hers and kept her eyes fixed on the snowy white tablecloth after that until, seconds later, as if someone had rung an inaudible bell, a plump lady appeared from nowhere, carrying a tray, her round face all smiles, her iron-grey hair pulled back in an elaborate twist. Puffing a little, she relieved herself of her burden, setting down cold orange juice, a steaming coffee-pot, hot toasted rolls wrapped in a linen napkin, her happy eyes giving Sarah a myriad sideways glances as if she was trying to see beneath her employer's new woman's dowdy exterior to find something exciting enough to explain the attraction.

Sarah was mortified. She coloured right up to the tips of her ears and had to fight to stop herself squirming with embarrassment as Francisco said mockingly, 'This is Rosalia. She speaks no English, but no tortuous incomprehensible introductions are necessary because she knows who you are.'

'Your latest woman—how disgusting you are!'

The moment the words were spat out she regretted them. She was supposed to be all weak and feeble—if her plan was to work—not fighting her corner, antagonising him. But he overlooked the outburst, pouring juice for them both, his voice silky smooth as he explained, 'Her son, Marcos, is busily learning your language. He plans to visit the States, where they have relatives who settled there a decade ago. But don't get any ideas about appealing to him, telling him of your plight, and asking him to smuggle you out in a laundry basket. It wouldn't work. Above all else, my staff are loyal.' He leaned back in his chair, turning the coffee-pot with the tip of one finger so that the handle faced her. 'Will you be mother?'

Her hopes were right down on the floor now. Clearly, he had no intention of releasing his prisoner on compassionate grounds, and she complied with his request to pour with ill grace, muttering sulkily, 'They must be loyal—or round the twist—to keep a great barracks of a place like this going on their own.'

She picked up her cup and buried her nose in it, feeling small when he informed her coolly, 'My home is not a barracks. And I will show you how beautiful it is when you are in a more agreeable mood. And I employ a full complement of staff, both for the house and the estates. The house staff, with the exception of Rosalia and Marcos, are on leave. It is an annual thing. I give them a full month. Rosalia will take her break later, visit with her married daughter and their children in the valley below while Marcos, as I told you, will visit the States. So you may finish your breakfast with a happy heart, knowing that my people are not treated as beasts of burden, their noses made nothing by your English grindstone.'

'My heart would be a whole heap happier if you let me go,' she riposted snappily. She'd had quite enough of pussy-footing around, and if that didn't suit her new neurotic persona then too bad. It wasn't working and she was heartily sick of the role in any case.

It was more than time everything was brought out into the open, not pushed away someplace where the sun didn't shine. And just thinking of the sun slicked her body with perspiration, beating down as it now was from the brilliant sky. She ran a hot finger round the neckband of her heavy cotton shirt and felt distinctly pale.

'You know I have no intention of letting you go,' he pointed out, idling back, one arm hooked lazily over the back of his chair. 'You are the ace in my pack. Without you, my leverage for forcing that lecherous old man to return my sister would be considerably diminished.'

There was no answer to that, not one she could think of right now, so she saved her breath then felt it catch unwillingly in her throat as he suddenly leaned forward, a concern that surely couldn't be completely manufactured narrowing his eyes.

'You are not eating, *señorita*. You are feeling ill?' His glance ranged over her pale moist skin, lingering on her slightly quivering mouth, but she wouldn't give him the satisfaction of knowing quite how much his concern touched her because it shouldn't touch her, shouldn't mean a thing. And it didn't.

'How do you expect me to look, in the circumstances?' she clipped. 'Radiant?'

She reached for a roll and spread it lavishly with honey. No wonder she felt peculiar; she had eaten nothing solid for twenty-four hours. Food was the last thing she had on her mind right now, but she forced herself, grumbling through a mouthful, 'You bring me here, lock me up and throw away the key. How do you expect me to feel?

'And what about my business? It's probably going to rack and ruin without me. When you finally let me go, I'll sue. For loss of freedom, and income, and—in any case——' she was warming to her subject and took another roll without thinking '—I too have a loyal staff. Jenny, for one, knows where I went. When I don't show up she'll get the Spanish authorities to make a search. I should be easy enough to track down.'

She stabbed the air in front of him to emphasise her point. 'There's the hotel receptionist in Arcos for one, the taxi driver who brought me here for another, not forgetting Dad's neighbour. I don't suppose she'll forget your face in a hurry—not the way she was giggling and bridling!'

She took a triumphant bite of her roll, watching for the apprehension that she was sure would dawn on the handsome face that fronted what must be a spectacularly empty brain. Had to be empty if he hadn't realised just how easily she could be traced once her disappearance became known, or even suspected.

But she slowly crumpled up inside when that slightly pitying smile flickered around the corners of his mouth as he informed her lightly, 'I phoned your office this morning, while you were catching up on your sleep. This Jenny you speak of was very understanding. Apparently, you contacted her yesterday afternoon and explained that you'd be away a little longer than expected.

'Anyway, when I told her who I was, reminded her that we'd met briefly in your office, explained that fate had brought you and I together again, that the need to be with each other was irresistible, that we were staying together, exploring the future possibilities of our affair, she became even more understanding. She even asked me to tell you not to hurry back, to assure you that she could cope— and said that I was a big improvement on the guy you had been dating.'

He flicked up a questioning brow. 'Serious, is it? Not to worry; I'm sure you'll be able to come up with something to soothe his ruffled feathers. I've noticed how inventive you can be. After all, you only need tell him the truth. But I wonder if he'll believe you?'

She wouldn't be telling Nigel Baines a single thing. That lukewarm relationship had been heading nowhere. So it didn't matter. The only thing that was capable of flooding her mind with grinding chagrin was the knowledge that he'd jumped one step in front of her again.

He could be very persuasive, him and that husky, sensually accented, dark, smoky voice of his. Jenny would have readily fallen for his explanation of a blinding grand passion, adding it to her own breathily rushed excuses of yesterday. A romantic at heart, Jenny would be soldiering on, dreamy-eyed, probably even getting as far as mentally selecting the outfit she'd wear to the wedding!

'You are the absolute pits!' she muttered, hateful tears stinging the back of her eyes. She tried to stem the threatened shameful flow, using her knuckles. She never cried. He couldn't make her! And it was all his fault.

She was hot and cross and she had dripped honey all down the front of her shirt, and she just knew he wouldn't give her the privacy to take it off and wash it through, sitting around in her bra while it dried. He would follow her like a damned shadow, that look of spurious caring on his face, then turn round and accuse her of showing herself off for his amusement and interest. And then he'd turn round again and tell her thanks but no, thanks; he didn't fancy what was on offer because who could fancy someone who looked like a bag lady? Or Chairman Mao! Oh, how she hated him!

'Don't.' His voice was a gentle dark velvet whisper as he took her hands away from her face. She shuddered, keeping her suspiciously moist eyes on the plate in front of her, feeling naked and vulnerable under that suddenly understanding, compassionate gaze. 'You mustn't be unhappy. Your father will get the message soon. In the meantime, relax. Enjoy what is here. There will be no more locks and there is much to see. It will only be for a little time. And who knows? You may find freedom of a different kind while you are here with me. The freedom to roam idly with me beneath the hot Spanish sun, to feel the warm, soft wind in your hair, on your face, your body, to enjoy the cool caress of a mountain stream, the seduction of fine wine as it slides down your throat, the scent of wild flowers borne on the wind. The freedom to savour what the moment offers, to find what is inside you...'

Sarah's eyes drifted shut, the tight lump in her throat relaxing away. That sensationally seductive voice, the things he was saying, reached right down into her subconscious, drawing out needs, fantasies she had never known she had, pulling her onwards to the point of mindless capitulation to the suggestions he was implanting. Almost, almost...

'And again, you might discover that I am not quite the monster you think I am. If you took the trouble to look deeper. I am here, right here with you.' His hands tightened on hers. 'Explore me.'

That did it. Brought her right back to her senses. Explore him? No, thanks! She wouldn't even demean herself by trying to figure out exactly what he meant. As she opened her mouth to tell him just that, he pushed the indignant words back down her throat by the simple expedient of closing her lips with one finger.

His touch scalded. Recovering from the shattering effects gave him time to rise to his feet and tell her, 'I must leave you for half an hour. No longer, I promise. Wait here, under the shade of the fig tree. I plan a small surprise.' His teeth gleamed whitely against her tanned olive skin. 'So think of that while you wait in the shade, listening to the music of the fountain, letting your senses be seduced by the scent of lilies, until I am ready for you.'

CHAPTER SEVEN

IF FRANCISCO thought for a single second that she would allow herself to be seduced by anything—lilies, or him!—then he would have to rethink his strategy. For strategy it most certainly had to be.

Sarah's eyes narrowed to dark blue slits as she took herself off to the shade of the enormous fig tree and determinedly closed her ears to the music of the water as it played in the ornate stone fountain. She had to think. To think hard and logically.

Sure now that he intended to confuse and disorientate her, she had to figure out how to anticipate him, and block each and every move he made. He had started out by treating her like his enemy, with cold, hard unforgiveness, switching to insults—like last evening when he'd practically eaten her with his eyes and then turned round and told her 'no, thanks'.

And the same thing had happened this morning. He had got her into such a state that, had he kissed her, held her, stroked her melting body, she would have mindlessly, weakly, allowed him to make love to her. Would probably have gone down on her knees and begged! But he'd calmly refused what he must have known was on offer, or could have been had he taken the situation a tiny step further, by telling her she looked like a bag lady!

Then, over breakfast, when she'd demonstrated that her fighting spirit was back to full strength, he had brought the power of that dark, sensual voice into play, talking of the warm wind on the mountains, of wine, of wild flowers—inviting her, if you please, to explore him!

She made a sharp, disgusted sound in the back of her throat and sat down on the slatted wooden seat that encircled the venerable old trunk, her legs thrust out in front of her.

Francisco Garcia Casals was working to a plan, she was certain of that. That he meant to seduce her she discounted after only a moment's consideration. She was too humble, too ordinary for a man such as he, a man who could surely have his pick of the world's most beautiful women. Not even the boredom of waiting for her father to respond could bring him to the point of wanting to make love to her to pass the time and lighten the tedium.

So the only sensible and logical explanation for his behaviour had to be his desire to confuse and disorientate her, get her to the point of not knowing whether she was coming or going, where she was at, too bewildered by the hard-and-soft, hot-and-cold treatment he was dishing out to have any mental energy left to figure a way of getting out of here.

To keep her locked in that suite of rooms for the duration would eventually rouse Rosalia's suspicions, so the only alternative course was to allow her limited freedom and keep his eye on her at all times. And, that being the case, it would suit him better to have her in such a disorientated state of mind that she would be too witless to cause any trouble.

A movement across the sun-drenched perfumed courtyard caught her eye. Rosalia clearing the breakfast-table. And taking her time about it. Had she been given orders to keep an eye on her master's 'guest'? Make sure she didn't go wandering off, get herself lost in the harsh Andalusian mountains?

Sarah wouldn't put it past him. In the same breath that he'd told her he was having to leave her on her own for half an hour he had tried to bemuse her with words. And had almost succeeded. He must have felt the need to use Rosalia as an unwitting guard, an extra form of protection.

Deciding to test her theory, she stood up slowly, then turned around and headed for the outer door set in the walls of the courtyard. Somewhere through there she'd find the great outer door.

It was easy enough to retrace the way they'd come yesterday afternoon, and she found the door. But it was locked, and she stood in the cool dim apartment, feeling completely trapped. As completely trapped as she'd been when he'd locked her in his suite of rooms.

Rosalia hadn't followed, either. Like her master, she would have known there was no way out. And the worst thing was, he had lied to her.

He had told her there would be no more locks. She couldn't imagine why she should have believed him in the first place. He was tricky and wicked, and she should have expected this. Instead, she couldn't remember when she had last felt so hurt; like the silence in the great chamber the tearing pain of it seemed to climb inside her and squeeze her heart until she wanted to cry out with anguish.

'Rosalia told me which way you'd headed.'

She hadn't heard his soft-footed approach, and stiffened, trying to mask the hurt in her voice, in her eyes as she whipped round to face him.

'You lied! You said there would be no more locked doors,' she accused him, unable to understand why this feeling of betrayal should intensify beneath his warm, darkly penetrating eyes, when, if she were sensible, she should have expected him to lie, taken it in her stride. And she hated the way his mouth curled into a slight, compassionate smile, as if he knew exactly how she felt. She couldn't bear the thought that he could come even close to reading the muddle of mixed emotions that were pounding through her head.

Her emotions, such as they were, had always been tidy, carefully controlled. That this man could churn them up, make them go haywire, shamed her. That he should know it demeaned her in her own eyes.

'Though I should have anticipated it,' she snapped out tartly, dragging herself back on track. 'For a man who would stoop to kidnapping a perfectly innocent stranger, what's a lie or two?'

She carefully avoided his eyes. He could make all her common sense, every last scrap of her cool control dissolve with one of those melting, disgracefully intimate glances of his; if she had learned anything from the past twenty-four hours, it was that. And she never forgot a lesson. But she couldn't avoid his voice.

'I'm sorry you're upset. It wasn't my intention.'

She shrugged, defending herself against the smoky drift of his words, denying, 'Who's upset? What's a locked door, set against all the other indignities? Oh! Let go of me!'

'Hush.' The hand that had taken hold of her arm slid down to entwine with her fingers now and somehow her loud objections got pushed back down her throat, making her feel giddy, stingingly aware of those strong fingers laced with hers. 'I have what I hope will be a pleasant surprise for you. And later we shall unlock all the doors. I will even show you where the keys are kept.'

Who did he think he was fooling? He was talking to her as if she were three years old. She snatched her hand away and dug in her heels. Show her where the keys were kept—so she could walk out of here any time she pleased? He must think she didn't have a brain in her head! And she didn't want his surprise, whatever it was. In her short but traumatic experience of him all his surprises had been grossly unpleasant!

He turned slowly, watching her, a tiny, annoying smile emphasising the sensuality of his heart-stopping mouth. And her face went red as she shifted her feet uncomfortably. She knew she looked a mess in her crumpled, sticky clothes but he didn't have to give the impression that he found her appearance verging on the hilarious, did he?

'Stop being mulish,' he ordered, his mouth tugging at the corners. 'Come peaceably, like the sensible lady you like to think you are, or be carried. It's all the same to me.'

Which left her no choice. And he knew it. Her greeny-blue eyes withering, she muttered, 'Only mental incompetents use their size to bully those physically smaller than themselves. Didn't anyone ever teach you how to ask nicely? Or wouldn't that suit your macho image?'

Which earned her the cold blast of his sudden black frown and for some reason she shivered, right down to her toes, and covered it quickly, grumbling, 'OK, I'm coming. Only don't expect me to be in the least bit interested in whatever you've cooked up. The only thing I'm interested in is seeing you behind bars. Where you belong.'

Which was hardly original enough to be truly cutting but it did stop him staring at her with that odd, frowning look in his eyes and got him moving, walking ahead down the long shady arcade, passing the door that led to the stairs to his suite and entering instead a cool sitting-room, quite magnificent, she noted absently as she trotted behind, with elegant furniture, softly coloured tapestries of enormous age, exquisite carved stone tracery in the deep window embrasures and great bowls of white lilies to perfume the air.

He took her on and through to a central hallway with a high vaulted ceiling and a floor of solid wood blocks polished to a glassy finish, and an awesomely Gothic, balustraded staircase, curving upwards, flanked at almost every step by gilt-framed portraits of oval-faced ladies in black, with pearls and fans and mantillas of awe-inspiring delicacy, and proud, gaudily uniformed officers on fine horses, displaying drawn swords and expressions just as ferociously arrogant as the throw-back who was leading the way.

The sheer size of the place, the quality, age and perfection of everything she saw had her mentally assessing the inexhaustible funds that would be necessary for the upkeep of such tasteful splendour. The income of the estates he'd spoken about provided the wherewithal, she supposed. Whatever, her father couldn't have picked a more formidable enemy if he'd set out to try.

She was on the point of asking how much further he expected her to trek when Francisco flung open a pair of double doors and led the way through to as feminine a suite of rooms as she could ever have imagined.

Delicate, inlaid furniture graced the sitting-room, the panelled walls painted white, the fabrics soft shades of varying blues with just the odd touch of pale primrose yellow for highlights, and beyond another set of polished wood double doors she caught a tantalising glimpse of an elegant four-poster, the lavish hangings in the purest white, festoons of lace and shimmering shot silk.

Was he about to offer her the use of this suite? She scarcely dared hope that he could be so thoughtful. The use of a pig-pen would have been accepted with gratitude—anything to get out of a repeat performance of last night, with him breathing down her neck, and quite literally, too, after he'd made her sleep in that bed with him.

But this suite was almost too much to hope for, and so it proved when he told her, 'These are Encarnación's rooms.' He gestured starkly, his mouth pulled down. 'Can you imagine a young girl not being happy here? Can you? As you see, she had everything she could have wanted. Why should she want to leave, run away with a libertine three times her age? Why?'

Black Spanish eyes bored into hers and his tension was evident in the taut bunching of his shoulder muscles, his wide-legged stance, the way his jaw tightened, his mouth a thin slash in the carved dark splendour of his features.

'How should I know?' Sarah muttered, her off-handedness a defence of sorts against the fierce black rage that sat so strangely in this delicately feminine room. 'Are these rooms your "surprise"? What am I supposed to do? Just look and make admiring noises, or move in?'

'When my sister returns she will not want to find a stranger using her room,' he returned with savage bite. 'You remain where I put you. With me. For the reasons I have already stated. *Entendido*?'

Brute! So much for those fleeting hopes. And he needn't think he could treat her any way he wanted, try to make her feel like nothing.

'Oh, silly old me,' she drawled, lowering her lids to hide her fuming eyes. 'For a moment back there I thought you were about to do the honourable thing. Or don't you know how?'

'Honour? What could you know about honour?'

As his black eyes condemned her she almost lost her precarious hold on her temper, but somehow managed to cling on to it, reminding him coolly, 'I am not my father, *señor*. Neither am I his keeper. And in my opinion you are just as unprincipled as he is. I am a totally innocent party in all of this mess yet you are keeping me here against my will whereas your sister, presumably, is with my father because she wants to be. Now, if I've seen whatever it was you meant me to see, may I leave? The air in the courtyard was marginally less oppressive. Out there I could almost believe I wasn't in prison.'

That piece of what he would regard as gross effrontery would probably earn her a spell in the dungeons, she thought, almost beginning to regret the spikiness of her tongue.

Dark, angry colour stained his high cheekbones and for a heart-tripping moment she thought he might hit her for reminding him that Encarnación had a mind of her own, had run away from home to be with Piers, was exercising her right to be with her lover. But then he smiled, suddenly, stunningly, and her eyes went wide as he actually apologised.

'Forgive me. You may be your father's daughter—and that is your misfortune—but you are right; you have done no harm to me or mine.' He spread his hands with disarming eloquence. 'I forget myself, *señorita*. You are, above anything else, a guest in my home. I beg a thousand pardons.'

The quiet dignity sent a surge of admiration through her. He had a cruel tongue when he wanted to use it, and the dictatorial arrogance was something else, way outside her experience. But there could be moments, like this one, when his chivalrous charm was brought into play, when she found herself actually liking him.

Which was a pity because he was her father's enemy, and he was holding her hostage, and that made him her enemy too, and not all the good-mannered chivalry in the world could excuse the way he had treated her.

Hardening her heart, she ignored his smile of contrition, suspecting laughter at her expense, a

suspicion that deepened when he gestured expansively towards a sofa at the far side of the pretty
room.

'See how thoughtful I can be, if I choose?
Come——' An imperious snap of his fingers in-
vited her to follow as he strode across the room.
'Beautiful clothes for a beautiful lady.'

Spurious flattery would get him exactly nowhere, Sarah decided grimly, staying exactly where
she was. Her looks had never been particularly important to her; they were an accident of birth. No
more, no less. She could look reasonably attractive
if she took the trouble to dress herself up but
'beautiful' she was not. And, as she could see now,
the delicate Empire sofa had clothing spread all over
it, soft fabrics in a multitude of gorgeous colours,
like a rainbow freshly fallen from the sky.

'Come and see. Don't tell me you're not
interested in having something other to wear than
that uninspired grey thing.'

She ground her teeth at the coaxing voice, the
laughing eyes. She hated the thought of being be-
holden to him for anything.

But she couldn't wear these trousers and shirt
until her father came charging to the rescue.

If he ever did.

Sooner or later, of course, he would get in touch
with his agent and receive that threatening message.
But it would probably be later, especially if he was
all bound up with his new young mistress, and in
any case he would probably prefer to keep
Encarnación than swap the exciting young love of
his life for his chronically disapproving daughter!

And hadn't she set out to prove to Piers that she was perfectly capable of looking after herself with no help, financial or otherwise, from him?

He would dismiss Francisco's threats, in the full knowledge that his prosaically level-headed daughter was perfectly capable of taking good care of herself.

Sighing, she walked slowly towards him, capitulating because she really had no choice. But not gracefully. She didn't owe him any grace.

'Where did you get this stuff from?' she enquired coolly, using her thumb and forefinger to pluck out what turned out to be a floaty, gauzy dress in soft fine cotton, white at the simple V-neckline, shading to deepest turquoise at the handkerchief hem.

'Where do you think?' The upward drift of one dark brow was expressive. 'From my sister's wardrobe. I do not dress in women's clothing behind locked doors.'

The idea was so laughable she almost smiled. But she wouldn't let herself. Making her mouth tight, she riposted grittily, remembering how appalled he'd been at the idea of her using—and presumably sullying—his precious sister's room, 'And won't Encarnación mind coming home and find a stranger wearing her clothes?'

He shrugged, his smile insolently arrogant. 'Why should she? She can throw them all away once you have used them. She has so many. She would have to live to be a hundred to wear them all. I picked out things that looked as if they would fit any size. Encarnación is more...generously built.'

Raw fury flickered over her features. There were too many insults in there for her to single out one and refute it. She was beginning to heartily dislike his wretched sister. Not only had she been stupid enough to get involved with Piers, so landing her up in this unholy mess, but she was increasingly coming over as a spoiled and over-indulged brat.

'Ah,' he murmured, completely misreading the direction of her wrathful thoughts. 'I intended no disparaging comparison. True, my sister is more bountifully endowed, but perfection of the female form—as you have already so generously shown me—does not depend on mere size.' Veiled eyes swept slowly, explicitly over her body and she felt her face burn with scarlet embarrassment. And something else: the hot melting sensation that swirled around deep inside her whenever he looked at her like that, spoke to her like that.

He was doing it deliberately, she thought chokily. And if she had any pride at all, even a smattering of that precious commodity, she would turn on her heels and walk right out of here. But he mesmerised her, took away her backbone, and she could only weakly stand and watch, gulping to ease her suddenly parched throat, trying to slow down her racing pulsebeats, as he turned and fluidly gathered up the pile of delicate garments, telling her in that wickedly husky voice of his, 'We go back to our room, yes? And there you can clothe yourself in a manner befitting the owner of a tantalisingly delectable body. And I will watch, and maybe I will find myself being tantalised beyond mortal endurance. Who knows?' His mouth quirked enticingly. 'Señorita Sarah might be transformed into a veritable Salome. I shall,' he ended loftily, 'be happy to give my verdict.'

CHAPTER EIGHT

'A VERITABLE Salome'—not if she could help it! A decade ago she had sloughed off that ridiculous name—along with the image that went with it. Erroneous, in her case, as he would soon see!

Stepping out of the shower, Sarah towelled herself dry, one eye warily on the closed door.

To her self-admitted amazement and never-ending relief, there hadn't been the expected need to fight her corner. Ending up back in his suite of rooms, she had sternly demanded privacy while she showered and changed. And he had calmly acquiesced, as if his disgusting earlier threat had not been made, the only proviso being that she didn't lock the door.

Which meant that he still thought she might do away with herself, she sighed, pulling on the clean underwear he had dropped on a stool earlier that morning. She was going to have to disabuse him.

Stringing him along had seemed like a good idea at the time, a foolproof ticket out of here because, she had figured, he wouldn't want her self-inflicted demise on his conscience.

Only events had proved he didn't have one, or only enough of one to make sure he kept his eyes on her at all times. And no way was she going to share his bed again. No way! So she would have to come clean. He would be furious when she explained how she'd made a fool of him. All that wounded Spanish pride didn't bear thinking about.

Yet it could work to her advantage, she comforted herself optimistically. He might even be furious enough to lock her up someplace else. Out of his sight. Which would be a darned sight more acceptable than having him forever hanging around, taunting her, insulting her, watching her, touching her...

The thought of him touching her made her feel decidedly giddy, as if every cell in her body was being whirled around in a giant mixer, her blood singing and throbbing round her body, leaving her brain starved of oxygen.

So she would think of something else instead. Such as what to wear. Pick the most sensible garment out of this bundle of froth and frivolity.

But there wasn't anything sensible to find—just silks and lace and cottons so soft and fine they were almost transparent. Trust a man to pick out unsuitable fripperies just because he liked the look of them, the feel of them as they slithered through his hands!

Pressured by the fear that he might get tired of waiting around while she made her selection, and decide to poke his head round the door to satisfy himself that she wasn't busily slitting her wrists, she scrambled into a wrap-over sheer cotton skirt in a delicate apricot shade and topped it with a sleeveless blouse in oyster-coloured silk. Then she discovered, too late to chop and change, that instead of demurely tucking into the waistband of the skirt the blouse was cropped revealingly short, ending just beneath her bosom, leaving her slender midriff bare.

Her cheeks went pink as she suspiciously examined her reflection in the mirror. And, just as she had feared, her image was the last word in femininity, her ash-blonde hair tumbling around her shoulders, the soft expensive fabrics hinting at the delicate curves beneath, her feet bare because for some ridiculous reason she couldn't bring herself to slip on the sensible flatties she had chosen to travel in. They would look hideous teamed with the things she was wearing.

And, she found to her inner disgust, she didn't want to look in any way hideous in his eyes. Not that she wanted to feel that way; she didn't. But there was nothing she could do about it for the moment. Tantalising: that was the word he had used, wasn't it? And tantalising simply wasn't her style. When she dressed up she preferred elegance and simplicity, not——

But at least she felt cooler and fresher and she could ask Rosalia to put her grey trousers and shirt in the washing machine. She needn't wear this sort of stuff all the time. And perhaps she could look for herself, borrow something more suitable from Encarnación's apparently limitless wardrobe. She would ask.

So she hooked the wings of her hair behind her ears, resolutely stuffed her feet into the black leather flatties and walked out, and he didn't look up from the papers spread out over the desk at the far end of the room until she edgily cleared her throat, the stern, brooding beauty of his profile making her unaccountably nervous now. And the nervousness increased to near panic when he did turn round, his smile too gorgeous to be borne, his eyes inviting her to drown in them.

'Beautiful, just as I predicted.'

His voice was a dark, sexily accented purr, which did nothing at all to help and her reaction to him made her despair, made her voice emerge as a sulky mumble as she plucked at the fabric of the floaty skirt and asked, 'Couldn't you have chosen something more practical? Jeans? T-shirts? I feel like a Barbie doll!'

'No, you don't. You feel adorable because you look adorable. Is that not so?'

He rose, sweeping the papers into a drawer and nudging it closed with a wickedly lean hip. 'Except for the shoes. We must see if something of Encarnación's might fit. As for the rest——' his dark eyes suddenly smouldered over her '—my sister is not like the rest of today's youth. You will not find Encarnación astride a moped, hanging around bars or discos. She has not been brought up to the ugliness of the ubiquitous jeans and T-shirts; she is feminine to the core, brought up to look and behave like a princess.'

A dark anger shimmered in his gaze and Sarah shuddered, sorting rapidly through what he had told her, her sympathies veering in Encarnación's direction for the first time. 'A princess', he had said. Shut away from reality in an ivory tower? Pampered and spoiled but allowed no real life of her own, no thoughts of her own? Little wonder she had taken to her heels.

All at once it no longer seemed to matter that she'd been forced to wear the other girl's clothes,

and the tiny frown that had formed between her
eyes deepened fractionally when the hard slash of
his mouth softened again as he told her, 'I'm sure
you're not in the least interested. Come, I promised
to open your cage, did I not?'

But she was interested. What she had learned
made sense of the way the Spanish girl had taken
it into her head to disappear with a lover old enough
to be her father—and then some.

Despite being pampered and protected all her life
she would have been normal enough to rebel, to
want to join in with whatever the rest of humanity
was doing. But she might well have been wary of
going it alone in the world outside her ivory tower,
warier still of relying on a boy of her own age to
guide her through the nitty-gritty of the real world.
But a much older man, a wealthy man, a man
who—as Sarah knew—could charm the female of
the species without even trying, then yes, she might
have seen Piers as a form of salvation.

Fully occupied with thoughts of the missing
Encarnación instead of brooding on her own predicament, she followed where Francisco led, barely
registering anything but the sound of their footfalls
as they descended the stone stairs and crossed the
main courtyard, blinking bemusedly when he unlocked the huge outer door and the harsh sunlight
illuminated the dim apartment.

'There,' he announced lightly. 'Your cage is open.
And here is where we keep the key.' He reached up
and placed it in a niche in the stone door surround.
'You need never feel you are a prisoner again.'

She raised her narrowed eyes to his, searching his
features for a hint of treachery; she found nothing

but a challenge, bright and glittering, and only understood it when he escorted her through an open doorway in the walled castle approaches to a sweeping terrace, dripping with wisteria, standing back from her the better to watch the play of emotions on her face, his own an awesomely handsome mask that didn't quite hide the devilish inner amusement.

The sort of freedom she had been hoping to gain in no way equated with the situation. She had been a fool ever to imagine that it would, to experience the quick, tight lift of excitement when he'd unlocked the door, told her where the key was kept.

Dry rocky mountaintops stretched away forever, severed deeply at the head of the lonely pass by an almost sheer drop of a thousand feet to the valley which sheltered the village.

Shielding her eyes against the shimmering glare of the sun, she could pick out the crumbled remains of the old castle walls, the groves of olive trees, the fields climbing upwards, clinging to the mountainside, each supporting neatly tended rows of crops, the higher areas of scrub home to herds of goats.

'And I suppose no one in the village knows a single word of English,' she said thinly, wilting beneath the fierce power of the sun high in the brassy blue sky.

There were wrought-iron seats on the terrace and she sank quickly down on one of them. Ever since he had tricked her into coming here she had been twisting her wits into knots, trying to figure out a way of getting away. But he had turned everything round, paid her back in her own coin—with interest—and she had never felt so despairing in her life. And she didn't need his lazily amused answer to tell her that the final hope had dissolved as quickly as a morning mist beneath the savage rays of the Spanish sun.

'No one. Few of them have ever ventured beyond the valley, or felt the need to. And most of them work on my estates. Besides, the road down is long and tortuous, and the road to the pass leads back to Arcos—and you know how far that is. In the other direction it goes only a little way into my estates, for transportation purposes. And the mountains are trackless.' He rocked back a little on the balls of his feet, just watching her, and she thought that he had never looked so dangerous, so in control of everything, herself included.

A shudder of anguish dredged through her. She could taste the danger, see it, hear its wordless, mind-numbing whisper, could almost name it for what it was.

She pushed herself back to her feet, hating herself for that momentary lapse into weak despair. What had she expected, for goodness' sake? A half-hourly bus service from the castle gates? After all, nothing had changed. Except that the walls of her prison had expanded somewhat.

She shot him a withering glare and he nodded, as if satisfied, and told her with a flashing smile of masculine superiority, 'Rosalia will be serving lunch in the courtyard in about an hour. Unfortunately, I shall be involved in estate business until this evening. I look forward to taking dinner with you. Until then, Sarah.'

A brief dip of his head and he was gone, but he left some of his powerful aura behind because for several long, heated minutes she couldn't think straight, pacing the stone slabs of the terrace distractedly, trying to work out what had changed. She knew something had, and didn't know what, or how, or when.

And once, just once, a glimmer of understanding flashed into her consciousness like the appearance of a shooting star in a black velvet sky, and she tired to catch it, to hold it, but it went, leaving her more distraught than before.

So, cross with herself, she gave up the attempt. Nothing had changed. How could it? She was letting the sun burn out her brain. She pulled herself firmly back together, walking quickly back the way Francisco had brought her, sitting in the shade of the arcade until Rosalia served her solitary lunch, making herself respond to the older woman's smiles, her unintelligible comments, forcing herself to consume the salad of hard-boiled eggs stuffed with prawns and ham, the cold rice dish intriguingly flavoured with anchovy, tomato and thyme, quenching her thirst with chilled, delicious white wine.

Which went some way towards helping her to thrust the unwelcome feeling of loneliness out of her head. Of course she wasn't missing his aggravating company. And of course she wasn't feeling abandoned because he had chosen to work. He had given her limited freedom, allowed her to see for herself how hopeless the idea of escaping on foot would be and, satisfied that he needn't bore himself silly by watching her every moment of the day, had taken himself off to involve himself in work—a far more interesting and rewarding project.

And she was glad, she told herself fiercely. Glad!

She took herself off to indulge in a siesta, giving herself a chance to get her mind sorted out, catch up on some of last night's missed sleep. She fell asleep almost as soon as her head hit the pillow in the sinfully comfortable bed, and woke in the late, golden afternoon, all nicely sorted out and knowing exactly how best to handle the horrible situation she'd been plunged into.

So she put her brain on hold as she washed yesterday's undies and put them on a towel-rail to dry, then had a shower, again, not knowing why she was bothering except that it helped to pass the time, and dressed in the clothes of Encarnación's she had worn earlier, not caring now that she didn't look in the least like her usual self.

Francisco had said that he would join her for dinner and she knew that that probably wouldn't be before nine in the evening, which gave her plenty of time to explore.

She stole like a shadow through lofty formal apartments, a magnificent ballroom, smaller, obviously family rooms where fires would be lit in the evenings when the cold wind scoured the mountaintops and the rain-swollen streams roared down the ravines. And she wondered how brother and sister spent their time here. Did they entertain? And what of their parents? Had their family been here for generations, right back to the Christian conquest? She wouldn't be at all surprised!

Thoughtfully, she made her way back to the central courtyard and, finding it empty, the sky darkening overhead, tramped back to his suite of rooms in her sensible shoes, trying to push the sensation of loneliness to the back of her mind, and didn't stop to examine the surge of relief that made her blood skitter light-heartedly through her veins when she walked through to the sitting-room and found him staring from one of the open windows, the mountain breeze ruffling his midnight hair.

He turned slowly, reluctantly almost, as she closed the door behind her. His eyes were brooding, the dark brows drawn down. He looked abstracted, she thought, as if he didn't know who she was, what she was doing here, and she wondered bleakly why that should hurt quite so much.

'Of course.' He shook his head slightly, as if dragging his thoughts back from outer space. 'Dinner. Rosalia and Marcos will bring it presently. I always dine here when I am alone.'

She nodded briefly, biting down on her lip, stifling the unexpected need to remind him that he wasn't alone. She was here, wasn't she?

But to all intents and purposes he was alone. She didn't count. He could extract a little amusement from her presence when he was in the mood to tease, insult or flirt. But he wasn't in the mood for amusement at her expense now, so her presence would simply be an irritant.

He must be deeply worried for Encarnación. Because he wanted to know she was safe and well, that she wasn't being hurt, being taught how to love only to discover she was merely one of an army of women who could count on nothing more than a fleeting, spasmodic place in Piers Bouverie-Scott's selfish attentions?

Or did his concern cut more deeply, more coldly? Had he had his own plans for Encarnación? A solid dynastic marriage perhaps. One that would not take place if the prospective bridegroom discovered how she had been spoiled. 'Spoiled' had been the word he had used.

Her bewilderment must have shown on her face because his eyes warmed suddenly, and he gave her a smile of such magnetism that her mouth went dry. Suddenly her hands were aching to reach out and draw his face down to hers, to kiss those sensual lips, drown in them, explore the secret of his masculinity, to kiss and be kissed until they were both beyond reason.

Horrified, she balled her hands into fists and pressed them rigidly against her side. Now she knew where the real danger lay! She had sensed it, sensed it strongly, but had been unable to name it. She could now. Her physical response to him, something she had never felt for any man before, was the danger. It had been there from the first, she recognised sickly, and was hourly growing stronger.

So she would be firm with herself, root it out. Kill it stone-dead. Remind herself what a louse he was. He was cruel, impatient, impossible, had the insolent arrogance of his personality stamped on every feature of that dark, brooding Latin beauty, a ferocious sexuality that had the power to stun...

Quickly, she slapped down the direction her thoughts were taking her in and, not looking at him because that mouth was still softened by that mind-stunning smile as he gestured her towards one of the sofas, said briskly, 'It's time for straight talking, I think.' She tugged the drifting wrap-over skirt demurely back into place and folded her hands in her lap to ensure that her long bare legs didn't inadvertently get back on display. 'Keeping me here isn't a joke, you know.'

'I didn't say it was.' That sexy mouth was still curling as he joined her on the sofa. 'I recognised the steel in you when I first saw you. I am not such a fool as to treat anything about you as a joke.' An arm snaked behind her, along the back of the sofa. 'In fact, I deeply respect your many and infinitely varied—qualities.'

Whatever that meant. She didn't think it would be wise to ask. He really was much too close. Sarah felt her entire body go quite rigid. Yet to move away would tell him that he affected her, and then the swirling danger would become something else again, something intolerable... She must project complete indifference. Somehow.

'Then perhaps you will respect what I have to say,' she uttered stiffly, blocking out the impulse to leap on to one of the other sofas. 'It could be weeks before Piers even gets your message. And then there's no guarantee he'll respond.'

'A man not respond to his daughter's plight? How could that be so?'

He was not taking her seriously. She could hear the laid-back amusement in his voice; it curled around her, stroked her, caressed her, crept into the very privacy of her soul. His hand moved slowly, taking a shining tendril of her hair between his long fingers, holding it gently, rubbing a little as if enjoying its silkiness. He was a supremely physical man...

'He doesn't even like me,' she muttered gruffly. 'We don't like each other. We're chalk and cheese. After my mother died he packed me off to boarding-school, but I did my best, when I saw him, to get him to moderate his behaviour. It didn't work out. Wine, women and work, never a thought to how embarrassing his behaviour—— Well,' she bit off, 'that's another story.' She wished he'd stop playing with her hair! It was...it was... 'The point being,' she spluttered nervily, 'he lives through all his five senses and he has spectacularly vivid senses, I might tell you. I prefer to use my mind and lead a tidy, professionally rewarding life. He won't renounce the pleasure of the moment for my sake. That's what I'm trying to get over to you.'

'No, that is not what you are trying to convey at all,' he said smokily, his fingers still intent on the enjoyment of what he was doing with her hair. 'You are trying to tell me that you have no emotions, no sensuality. That you are a properly programmed robot, without a sex. Is that not so?'

He edged a little closer, his fingers sliding up to her scalp, turning her head, making her face him, making her recognise the unholy silver gleam deep in those lustrous black eyes. 'Well, protest away, Salome, but I know better. I know all about passion, therefore I can recognise it easily. It sang out to me; I saw it throbbing inside you, fighting to get out of that enforced sexless exterior on only our second encounter.'

His fingers were warm on her scalp, stroking, gently kneading, and she twisted her head away, her face going scarlet as she snapped out, 'Don't call me that! It's not my name; my name is——'

'Salome,' he interrupted with lazy amusement, capturing her bristling body with his hands, sliding them up to fasten round the naked skin of her midriff. 'It's more appropriate than you like to think. Shall I demonstrate?'

No! Her brain said no, but her mouth wouldn't function. How, for pity's sake, could she expect it to when his fingers were edging beneath the oyster silk, finding the full undercurve of her breasts, lingering there, her lacy bra no barrier at all?

He moved closer and she stopped breathing as tiny flickers of sexual tension quivered all over her body and exploded in a million shattering shards of wild sensation as the pads of his fingers found the taut nipples and began to tease them.

There was fever in her blood, wicked and wild and wanton. It was burning her up and she felt sweat break out from every pore, slicking her body, and with a groan of utter helplessness she slithered towards him, writhing, winding her arms around his neck; his head came up, his mouth so close to hers that she could feel the heat of it, the passionate heat, taste and savour the kiss that surely had to come, and someone knocked on the door and she went into shock, her eyes wide with the wildness of knowing how deplorably she'd behaved.

He straightened up slowly, his smile conspiratorial and lazy as he removed one hand to rest it gently against her knee, replacing the other along the back of the sofa as he instructed, *'Entre.'*

She had never, ever been so pleased to see anyone in the whole of her life as she was to see Rosalia and, presumably, her son Marcos. She could actually breathe again, albeit shakily, as the two of them set the covered dishes they were carrying, on trays that looked as large as barn doors, neatly and efficiently on a table in front of one of the windows.

Shifting along the sofa, as far away as she could get from that long, lean, scorchingly sexy body, she slapped his hand away from her knee and hoped she didn't look as hectic as she felt. But very much feared that she did when, as Francisco got fluidly to his feet and strolled over to the table to open the wine, saying something in a dusky undertone to Rosalia, Marcos gave her a long and strangely complicated look.

He wasn't much above eighteen, slightly built, very dark, with almost girlish features, but that look was nothing but pure male speculation. A mystifying mixture of approval and disapproval. And only when he turned back to what he'd been doing did the penny drop.

Rosalia would have gossiped about their employer's new mistress, closeted up in that princely suite of rooms. That quick, revealing assessment had said quite plainly that her status wasn't approved of, but her fluttery feminine appearance was. Oh! It was all too much!

And that was why the louse had touched her up! To get her all in a dither to reinforce the reason he'd given his staff for her presence here. If she'd been sniping and snapping at him, sitting on the opposite side of the room, his cover would have been blown!

Next time he tried that on again she'd be good and ready for him. Ready to slap his head until it flew off his shoulders!

'Come. Eat. Drink.' The dark drawl was like a punch in the solar plexus, making her poor head spin. But when he added, investing his voice with sinful meaning, 'We shall not be disturbed again tonight,' she was able to hang on to herself and remind herself tartly of what happened to little girls who met up with the big bad wolf.

And it most certainly wasn't going to happen to her. She knew exactly what to say to cool his spurious ardour, make him forget his idle desire to have a little fun at the expense of silly Sarah Scott.

Gratifyingly cool now, she set her face and joined him at the table, letting him help her to the various dishes, even though she had completely lost her appetite. Then, when he was seated, and before he could start saying things, things that would get her all hot and bothered again, she calmly began her defensive attack.

'As you seemed unable to believe that Piers won't come running to my rescue with your tearful, repentant sister on his arm, may I put it to you that she would probably refuse to set foot inside this place again?'

Keeping her face stony, her eyes on the stem of her wine glass as she twisted it round and round in her fingers, she refused to let the sudden dark silence from the opposite side of the table affect her in the slightest. He had asked for it.

'After all,' she went on, 'there can be little doubt now that she and Piers are an item. She is probably revelling in the freedom to be a woman instead of a cardboard princess, the owner of more frilly clothes than she could ever wear, shut away from the wicked, contaminated world in lovely, lonely

isolation. Why should she come back when there
is nothing here for her? When someone is actually
teaching her how to live?'

'You condone what that old man has done to
her?' He slammed his cutlery down on his plate
with a violence that had her jumping out of her
skin. She glanced up at him quickly. His anger was
so cold, it froze her bones. But at least it had
stopped his sexual overtures, and that, for her peace
of mind and self-respect, was the only thing that
mattered.

'No,' she returned levelly. 'I can't. His affairs—
as you said once yourself—are legendary. But up
until now, and as far as I know, always with older,
mature women. Widows, mostly.'

'Widows?' he scorned bitingly. 'Are you forgetting Liberty Torrence? Her third husband—or
was it her fourth?—threw her out when her affair
with your father hit the headlines.'

Forget? How could she ever forget that public
humiliation?

It had been around twelve months after her
mother's death when the pictures of her father and
the famous film actress in a more than compro-
mising situation had been splashed all over the front
pages of the tabloids. She'd just been elevated to
dormitory prefect, her good behaviour, politeness
and application to her work impressing her teachers.
And she could still hear the giggles, the lewd comments whispered behind her fellow students' hands,
see the embarrassing newsprint pictures pinned up
over her bed. That, as much as the shambolic life
she and Patience had led as they'd pandered to
Piers' genius, had made up her mind never to allow

her emotions to play any part in the way she ran her life.

And she was not about to alter that rule now.

Staring him straight in the eye, she continued, as if his input had no meaning, 'You're worried about her, I understand that. And I agree, it's unfortunate that she ever met up with Piers. But you and your parents must take some of the blame. If she hadn't been—and you admitted this yourself—so protected, it wouldn't have happened.'

'You presume too much, *señorita*!' He thumped his fist on the table, making the glasses leap. 'Encarnación and I have no parents. For the past five years since our mother's death I alone have been responsible for her. I have brought her up as our mother would have wished. I inherited my father's genes—and I am proud of them. But for Encarnación—they must not touch—that was our mother's wish. It would not have been fitting for her to be fired by our father's gypsy blood. We had to be careful that she didn't catch the infection. Yet you sit there in judgement, presuming to tell me she was wrong. I was wrong!'

Anger turned his dark velvet voice into a menacing growl, turned his eyes into weapons. But Sarah kept her head. He didn't frighten her. She tipped her head consideringly to one side, careless of the way it made his black frown deepen. So his father had been a gypsy. That was interesting. It explained his volatile temperament, surely? She would ask him about it, but some other time, when he wasn't so likely to snap her head off.

Telling herself that her deep interest in everything about him was merely academic, she felt a quiver of something quite terrifying scatter the blood in her veins as he leapt up from the table, his mouth grim, telling her, 'I have had more than enough of this day! I am going to my bed.' He reached for her arm, dragging her off her feet. 'You too. I order it. And do not so much as say one word. Not one! The consequences, I promise, would not enthral you!'

CHAPTER NINE

HE'D had more than enough of this day! Did he think she hadn't? Did he think he had the monopoly on fierce emotions? If anyone should be throwing a temper tantrum, it should be her!

Sarah had a mind to do just that. It might even be fun, she thought belligerently as he hustled her through to the adjoining bedroom. And he didn't really think that he could force her to keep her mouth shut, like a little grey mouse in a corner, just because he hurled threats at her in his temper, did he?

Her eyes sparking defiance, she picked his imprisoning fingers off her arm, one by one, and opened her mouth to tell him he needn't think she was going to share that bed with him again, because she wasn't, but the steel in his hooded black eyes, the thunderous warning of his frown pushed the words right back where they'd come from.

All that barely contained black anger, just because she'd had the temerity to point out that his over-protective, chauvinistic attitude towards his sister's upbringing was probably the underlying cause of her defection!

And his fierce inner rage wasn't frightening her. She met his gaze and held it, glittering aquamarine squaring up to savage black. On the contrary, she decided as her breath snagged in her throat, he had never seemed more vulnerable to her than he did at this moment. And, taking her by complete surprise, her heart did a little leap then melted inside her. She wanted to wind her arms around him, assure him that everything would be all right. Kiss him better.

She deeply amazed herself.

She picked one of the pillows off the bed and told him gently, 'I'll sleep on one of the sofas. I'll be perfectly comfortable. Shall I use the bathroom first, or will you?'

His snort of disgust told her he wasn't amused and he plucked the pillow from her fingers and tossed it back where it belonged, his mouth tight as he uttered, 'I warned you: no arguments. Nothing.'

'But——'

'Not a word!'

Kiss him better? That was a laugh! How could she have been such a wimp? She wanted to hit him until he begged for mercy! Planting her hands on her hips, her chin at a haughty angle, she returned his glare with interest and clipped out coolly and clearly, 'You are bigger than I am and much stronger, but that does not—and I repeat, *not*—give you the right to bully me.'

She watched his hard mouth tighten, the aristocratic nostrils pinch with irritation, and somehow knew she could push her luck. He wouldn't harm a single hair of her head, despite all the fire and fury.

'I understand why you insisted I—er—sleep with you last night. But your concern was based on a misunderstanding. I went to the roof to get a breath of air. I couldn't sleep. I had no intention of leaping off the battlements—I'm not that feeble.'

She sucked her bottom lip between her teeth, wondering whether it would be wise, considering his present mood, to point out that she'd successfully made a fool of him. Then, seeing his face go totally impassive, a black brow arching upwards in what seemed like contempt, she decided to go for broke.

'You misunderstood and I played along with that in the hope that you might have a conscience and let me go. Obviously I was wrong about that. However, you can rest assured that I won't do anything foolish. Therefore there is no need to have me sleeping alongside you.'

'You talk like a piece of business correspondence,' he said impatiently, crossing his arms high over his impressive chest. 'How do I know you are not lying again? You bleated about locked doors, so I——' he made an expansive gesture with one hand '—unlocked all. I humoured you. In return you will humour me.' It was not a request, it was a command armoured with plate steel. 'I can't take the risk of trusting you to behave yourself.'

'You left me alone for most of the day,' she returned, deploring the tinge of a whine in her voice, wondering where it had come from.

He answered with evident boredom, 'I asked Rosalia to keep an eye on you—letting her know I was afraid you'd get bored without my constant attentions. She was to tell me immediately if you showed signs of restlessness, and then I would cease my work at once and rush to entertain you. She reported, later, that you'd eaten a good lunch and were sleeping peacefully in our room.'

'Devil!' she spluttered. What must that make her in Rosalia's eyes? A mindless dolly-bird who got in a huff if she didn't have a man around, dancing attendance! Her reaction earned herself a grim smile.

'Exactly. And now you know what you are dealing with, perhaps you will stop annoying me and do as you're told for once. I have been too kind to you, allowed you to get above yourself. So try to remember your position here.' He made an impatient gesture with one hand. 'Use the bathroom and get into that bed. I do not want to put myself to the trouble of manhandling you there, and tying you to the posts. But be assured that I will, if necessary.'

The snap of black temper in his eyes told her he meant exactly what he said. It didn't bear thinking about. Her stomach churning as if she'd just taken a roller-coaster ride to Hades, she stamped to the bathroom, muttering darkly under her breath.

But he wouldn't stay awake all night, she told herself as she savagely brushed her teeth. He might make her get in that bed, but he couldn't stop her creeping out again as soon as he was asleep.

Getting into her torn nightie was hardly a joy, and as he'd been the one to tear it he might have had the decency to supply her with something of Encarnación's. Sighing crossly, she held the ripped edges together and sidled out into the bedroom, her heart pattering around, only relaxing a little when he stalked past her and closed the bathroom door without so much as a word or even a look.

Scurrying to the sitting-room, she grabbed an armful of cushions and scampered back to place them in a straight line right down the centre of the bed then leapt beneath the light covers. As a barrier it wouldn't take much dismantling, but she would instantly know if he tried to remove them, and take immediate evasive action.

Squeezing her eyes tightly shut, she turned her face into the pillow, her ears straining to pick up the sounds that would tell her he'd returned to the bedroom. She would kill Piers with her own bare hands—save Francisco the bother—for getting her into such an intolerable situation! She then spent a long time wondering where all her prized control had gone, pondering on how easily a given set of circumstances could present her with a bucketful of raw emotions she was beginning to find increasingly difficult to control.

Given set of circumstances! she scoffed at herself, punching the pillow. Who did she think she was kidding? She had never come within a whisker of losing a scrap of her careful control through all sorts of difficulties, be they with her impossible father, over-demanding clients or ultra-pedantic bank managers, until she had come up against this Spanish devil! And the fact that he was holding her hostage had nothing whatever to do with it, she recognised, hating him all the more for that uncomfortable truth.

It was the way he made her feel, just by looking at her. And when he actually touched her she went completely haywire, she acknowledged under direct and painful self-examination. A chemical reaction which had never come near to occurring with any other man, and one she could do precious little about.

All she could do was to work hard at hiding it, and as she had never been afraid of hard work she supposed it shouldn't present a problem she would be incapable of handling. What had happened earlier this evening would not be repeated. She had been taken unawares that time. In future she would be rigidly on guard. And whether Piers responded to that message or not Francisco couldn't keep her here indefinitely. Nothing lasted forever.

On that hopeful thought she settled more comfortably but the unmistakable click of the bathroom door closing, the small sounds he made as he moved around the bedroom had her as tense as piano wire, every cell in her body on red alert as she waited for the inevitable.

She heard his soft-footed approach to the other side of the bed, and then the humphing sound he made in his throat as he pulled back the cover. Presumably because he'd noticed the barrier—and was showing his contempt for its flimsy nature?

Doing her best to pretend that she was already deeply asleep, she felt the mattress dip as he slipped in beside her. Leaving the cushions where they were, he turned on his side and clicked off the light and the moment she heard his breathing relax she fell asleep as if someone had pressed a switch inside her head.

Sarah flopped over on to her tummy as she began to come awake, an outstretched hand pushing against the barrier of cushions. And just for a moment, before she opened her eyes to the golden morning light, she experienced a deeply slicing pang of regret for the distance Francisco had been quite happy to leave between them.

The assimilation of that piece of self-knowledge brought her fully awake immediately and she twisted round and sat up in a hurry, anguished eyes scanning his side of the bed, the room. No sign of him. Drawing in a shaky breath, she pulled the covers up to her chin and forced herself to look the unpalatable facts squarely in the face.

That regret, the nature of it, had presented itself before she'd been properly awake. So it had been uncensored. It had been the unvarnished truth.

Subconsciously she had wanted him to hold her, cuddle her close, as he had on the previous night. And had she actually wanted more than that? Very much more?

Frowning, she pushed that conjecture aside. It was unproven. And she had enough to cope with without adding idle speculation to the burden of knowing she had wanted him to toss the cushions out of the bed and tug her into the curve of his body.

You are, she warned herself sternly, in serious trouble, lady.

She felt herself flush with the shameful embarrassment of her knowledge when Francisco walked through the door. Her heart leapt at the mere sight of him, though there was nothing 'mere' about him, she acknowledged as she tried unsuccessfully to will the tide of fiery colour to recede.

Dressed all in black this morning, he was unfairly spectacular and the smile he gave her wasn't lacking in that department either, because it made her toes curl, sent a shiver of sensation that was decidedly delicious all the way down her back. Unfortunate physical manifestations of a malaise she didn't quite know how to treat, she decided uneasily.

And he wasn't helping because his voice was warm and sunny, his accent riveting, as he came over to the bedside, put a glass of chilled orange juice in her hands and said, 'This morning we will walk before the sun gets high. We both need the exercise.' He dipped his head to one side, his eyes wandering over her flushed features. 'We shall take our breakfast with us—I have already told Rosalia. Hurry now; drink your juice.'

The grin he gave her made her head swim; she clutched the glass tightly with both hands because she felt giddy enough to spill the contents and she watched him, mesmerised, as he strolled over to the wardrobes and riffled through the clothes he had decided his sister wouldn't miss.

His black mood of the night before had gone as if it had never been. He was impossible, unpredictable, a devil. She never knew how he would be with her from one moment to the next, and her eyes were wary as he selected a hanger and draped something in peacock-blue filmy cotton over the foot of the bed. His sinfully beautiful mouth was curling at the edges as he told her softly, 'Wear this; it will cover you adequately. You must treasure your beautiful, delicate skin, protect it. You are not like me, a gypsy, to walk uncovered in the sun. So no more anger between us, eh, Salome? Today we will be friends.'

Oh, a devil indeed! After the chilling anger of the night before she felt as if she had walked into brilliant sunshine. And he was getting more Spanish by the second, she thought wildly as she watched him watching her from lazy black eyes, his long-fingered hands planted on his sexily lean hips.

She would have given at least two of her teeth for the strength of will to command him to go away, to take himself for a walk and forget to come back. But she doubted there was a woman alive who could resist him and knew he was aware of it, but even that failed to put a stop to her willingness to fall in with any plans he had made. And she hadn't even inwardly objected to his use of her given name, she thought, more in sorrow than in anger, watching him as he took the empty glass from her limp fingers then walked out into the adjoining sitting-room, the smile curving his lips telling her plainly that he knew he could get his own way, whatever the opposition.

Only she wasn't opposing him, was she? she thought as she clambered out of bed and into the bathroom, excusing herself on the grounds that there seemed little point in getting stubborn about this because a walk would pass the time, and she could do with the exercise, and, anyway, her father might have turned up by the time they got back.

But she didn't believe that, did she?

However, she refused to think about that, or anything else, as she slid the soft fine cotton over her head, and didn't scowl at the ultra-feminine reflection the mirror threw back at her because the simple loose style, the cool V-neckline and floaty sleeves that came down to her wrists felt good. And the colour suited her, dramatically darkening her aquamarine eyes, making her hair even paler, glossier.

She walked back into the bedroom, her breath escaping on a tiny gasp when she met the gleaming approval of his eyes as he wandered back through from the other room.

The things he could do to her with his eyes alone shouldn't be allowed, not in a civilised society, she thought raggedly, then decided he wasn't civilised at all, not really, because beneath the handsome, groomed exterior, all the laid-back charm he seemed able to turn on at will, lurked a bundle of primitive passions that could explode without warning, a truly arrogant belief in his own omnipotence, a raw vitality that made every other man she knew seem congenitally anaemic and a ferocious sexuality that had the power to stun.

He was holding a wide-brimmed straw hat and as he advanced she felt her bones turn to water. She said chirpily, trying to rally herself, 'Is that for me?' and lost the little ground she'd gained for herself when his slow mocking smile, the unholy gleam in his eyes rendered her incapable of speech or movement.

'I guess it must be. It's not quite my style; doesn't do a thing for me.'

He moved closer and put it on her head, tugging gently on the wide brim to achieve the effect he wanted, smoothing away soft tendrils of hair, and all the time he was much too close and she had to fight a terrible craving to move a little closer still, close enough to feel that magnificent, vital body touching hers, imprinting her flesh with the magnetic potency of his.

She closed her eyes on a wave of despair. The fight was well and truly on—the fight with herself. What she felt was lust, a wild stirring of hormones too long ignored. She would not give in to it. She would not follow in her father's hedonistic footsteps. She would not lose control. Not even for a moment!

'Shall we go?' She twisted her head away and tried to look frosty but her efforts only served to amuse him. She saw the half-hidden smile as he picked up a canvas bag she hadn't noticed before and hoisted the strap over his shoulder.

'Breakfast.' He patted the bag lightly. 'As I told you, I asked Rosalia to pack a picnic.'

He looked impossibly smug and quite extravagantly gorgeous and she wanted to kick him for the way he made her feel. But she had decided not to dwell on that, hadn't she? So she told him tartly, 'How thoughtful. But then I suppose thoughtfulness comes easily when you can pay somebody else to do the donkey work.'

'Friends—remember?' His voice was a throaty, velvet purr and his hand was on her waist as he led her out of the suite. Her brows peaked, expressing a vague anxiety that came out of nowhere, as they made their way down through the sturdy stone building, ending up on the wisteria-clad terraces where he'd left her the day before.

Friends. She would like to think he was her friend, she thought wistfully as he ran lithely down a flight of stone steps at the far end of the terraces and pushed open a narrow door in the curtain wall.

In fact, she craved his friendship quite desperately, she acknowledged, his smile hitting her like a blow to her chest as he held open the door that led on to the mountainside.

But it wasn't possible. How could they be friends after what he'd done? He had tricked her into coming here and would hold her here, depriving her of her freedom, until he got what he wanted—Piers' neck beneath those strong tanned hands, she reminded herself. And as if that weren't enough he had humiliated, insulted and embarrassed her. So no, they couldn't be friends, and she couldn't understand why she should want it otherwise.

She deplored the way her throat suddenly tightened, tears stinging the back of her eyes. She didn't know what was wrong with her, and gave up trying to fathom it out when he held out a hand to help her over the stony path.

Just for today she would pretend, she capitulated as she felt those lean fingers curl around hers, give way to the unexpected side of her nature that seemed intent on fighting the calm control that had been the cornerstone of her existence. She didn't want a battle, not today, not when the warm Andalusian wind was moulding the fine cotton to her strangely sensitised flesh, the scent of wild herbs and flowers a heady narcotic, drugging her senses, the view of the dry rocky mountains almost as magnificent and soul-stirring as the unpredictable Spaniard who gripped her hand so tightly, fierce pride in his black eyes as he pointed out the extent of his lands.

'Has all this been in your family forever?' she asked, flustered, as he sank to the sparse dry grass at the foot of a rocky outcrop, pulling her with him. Today she was allowing the fantasy of friendship and that probably explained the burning need to know all about him. Friends needed to know what made each other tick, didn't they?

'Practically,' he answered with a tiny shrug. 'At least, to an offshoot of my mother's branch of the family. My mother had blotted her copybook as far as her family were concerned. I inherited a place that was rapidly falling into ruin, estates that were run-down and under-utilised, simply because there was no one else.' Again the tiny shrug and all the time he'd been talking he'd been rummaging in the capacious haversack, producing a simple meal of bread and ham and olives, a flask of hot coffee.

'Nothing's ruined now,' she probed, accepting the slice of ham he offered on the tip of a wicked-looking knife, folding it in her fingers, watching him as he cut a slice for himself.

His thick black lashes lowered, hiding his expressive eyes, he answered levelly, 'I made sure it is not. I look after what is mine to the full extent of my talents and energy.'

As he had looked after his sister? she wondered. Jealously, smotheringly, eventually driving her away with someone as unsuitable as Piers?

But he cut off the direction of her thoughts, telling her, 'I gave up dealing on the international money market and gave everything I am to the task of putting everything here back together again. Making it pay. And that's the name of the game, isn't it, Salome?'

His smile was sweet and slow, drawing her closer into the web of his attraction, and she dipped her head, hiding behind the wide brim of her sun hat, overcome with a completely novel sense of shyness. And she felt her insides quiver as he said softly, 'We've been too busy scoring points off each other to share confidences. Understandable, perhaps, in the circumstances, but I want it to stop. I want us to get to know each other. I hope you want it too. So tell me something about yourself, and take your time. We have all day.'

He wanted to get to know her, and they had all day! So this wasn't to be a short break, breakfast sandwiched between a little essential exercise, then a return to the castle where he would leave her to kick her heels all day under the watchful eye of Rosalia. She went weak inside, almost melting with excitement at the thought of it, and said huskily, 'What's to tell? I'm a very ordinary person.' She popped the last morsel of food in her mouth, hardly able to swallow it because of the tightening of her throat muscles.

'Not so ordinary.' He stretched full-length in the shade, his arms crossed behind his head, closing his eyes. 'You're the most intriguing woman I've ever met. Layer upon layer. Stubborn as they come. Were you a difficult child?'

She smiled and shook her head. Then, realising he had his eyes closed, she said, 'I was very biddable. I had to be. The only one in our family allowed to be difficult was Piers. Patience—my mother—and I used to run around after him doing our best to bring some order into his life, making sure he ate and slept fairly regularly and sometimes changed his clothes.'

He was easy to talk to. Perhaps because he wasn't looking at her, maybe drifting off to sleep. She tucked her legs beneath her, her skirts pooling around her, turning her head to watch an eagle soaring high above the picturesque village in the valley so far below, not looking at Francisco because now it hurt too much, an unbearable pain clutching at her heart.

She flinched at the sudden harshness in his tone as he demanded, 'Was he unfaithful to your mother? Was that why you tried to become cold?'

Cold? Was that what he thought of her?

'I've never consciously tried to be anything except sensible,' she replied, stung. 'Somebody has to be when you're living around my father. He earned himself a reputation by his painting, and an even bigger one by horsing around. I watched Patience run herself ragged and after she died I tried to carry on the good work. But I was only a kid. There was no way I could succeed where she had failed.

'And I don't know whether he was unfaithful.' Her fingers were busily pleating the fabric of her skirt, her voice going tighter. 'If he was, Patience hid it. He used to take himself off, usually when he'd been working non-stop on a painting, and, as Patience put it, let off steam. It was only after her death that his flings with other women became public knowledge.

'Perhaps,' she added slowly, with a shaft of insight, 'perhaps he missed her. Found substitutes for a short time, but wouldn't put any one of them permanently in Patience's place because none of them could live up to his memory of her.'

She chewed uncertainly on the corner of her lip. 'I don't know. I don't think Dad and I have ever really talked about anything important. But I do know that his women were all round about his own age. Maybe mothering—which was what Patience had been doing all their married lives—was what he was looking for. As well as passion.'

Which was why, at the very beginning, she'd been unable to believe that he'd taken up with a girl younger than his own daughter.

'So you decided to make your life tidy and ordered, in direct contrast to the chaos you probably believed was responsible for your mother's untimely death. A natural reaction from a sensitive child in her teens.' Suddenly his arm snaked up and fastened around her neck, drawing her down beside him on the herb-scented grass, his voice a wicked whisper as he said, 'The repression didn't go too deep to do permanent damage, did it, Salome?'

Somehow one of his hands was resting lightly on her breast, his fingers softly curling, and her body took heat from the closeness of his, the wild race of hot blood through her veins making her insane with need for him as, his lips moving slowly, erotically against hers, he murmured, 'Let me repair the tiny damage. Let me show you what passion means.'

CHAPTER TEN

'I DON'T think——'

Sarah tried desperately hard not to melt right into him; her faltering words of attempted protest felt clumsy, thick in her throat, and he silenced her, his lips covering hers, murmuring, '*Bueno*. I don't want you to think. Simply to feel. Give yourself up to sensation.' His mouth moved over hers like hot velvet and her lips quivered helplessly for one fraught, indecisive moment before her long lashes drifted down as she closed her eyes, accepting the sweet release of inevitability.

A deep hunger grew and raged within her, an aching unquestionable need to belong to this man, body, soul and heart, an instinctive, primeval knowledge that this was right, that nothing beyond this unbearably sweet moment mattered. And the way he was touching her breasts, stroking them through the thin fabric of her borrowed dress, went beyond torment; she arched her body in frantic need and heard him whisper thickly in his own language, his body hardening as his kiss changed from sweet seduction to dark, driven passion.

He was utterly dominant, his lips, his tongue, his hard male body demanding submission now and she gave it willingly, lost to rational thought, winding her arms around his neck, instinctively inviting, lost in a welter of savage emotions as she wrapped her long legs around his, binding him closer. His hands shaped her body with a burning urgency that electrified her senses and made her cry out his name on a sigh of aching need.

And when his hand slipped beneath the rucked-up hem of her dress and touched her, slid lingeringly over the soft, satiny skin of her thigh, she gave a tiny gasp, moving her hips against his, shocked by the undreamt-of world of pleasure that was opening up for her.

'*Dios*!' For a moment his body went rigidly still and she could hear the heavy pumping of his heartbeats, and then he released her, twisting away, his slashing cheekbones stained with the hot flames of desire, as intense as the blistering Spanish sun as it rode the raw blue sky.

Sarah blinked bewildered eyes, crossing her arms over her tummy where an aching emptiness was rapidly taking the place of that melting loveliness, and her tiny mew of distress was instinctive, the sound torn from the depths of her being.

He gave her a quick, searching frown then took one of her hands in his, raising it to his lips, murmuring thickly, 'No, no, *querida*. This is not rejection. Never think that. I burn for you; my whole body is on fire for you.' He pressed slow kisses on the backs of her fingers, holding her captive with his hot black eyes. 'If you only knew how hard I had to fight not to take what I want so desperately. You are beautiful, passionately generous, adorable, and I want you more than I can remember ever wanting any woman. But now is not right.' He turned her hand, his lips moving lingeringly on her palm. 'Though the time will come, and it will be perfect for us, this I promise you.'

She dragged in a breath as the madness receded, leaving her feeling almost stunned, then scrambled unsteadily to her feet. She didn't doubt him. It would be perfect between them, shatteringly so.

But the chill wind of reason was cooling her blood, clearing her mind. She craved him, all of him, with everything in her. Quite suddenly, he was the centre of her existence. And if this was what love was, then it terrified her. It took away her sense of self, her identity, and wrapped it up with him so that there seemed no place to go, not without him, nowhere to be but by his side.

He had kissed her and she had been swept away in a whirlwind of insanity, the madness of falling in love, the crazy desire to cleave to him through the rest of her life. It was only his control that had enabled her to rescue hers. She saw it all with a clarity that hurt.

He would make love to her when the time was right. Reason and logic made that promise feel like a threat. And how would it be? When would the time, the place be right? Chilled champagne, the big soft bed, the dark velvet, exotically scented Spanish night? And then what? Boot her out again when he got bored, or when her father showed up, whichever came the sooner?

She wasn't going to let herself compound the hurt that was already squeezing her heart until it bled. She had more sense than that.

'I'll make my own way back,' she said coolly, not looking at him. 'Carry on walking, if that's what you want. I won't get lost. We haven't come far.' Not come far! she thought on an aching shudder. She was a million miles away from the unawakened woman who had so blithely set out this morning, pretending to herself that she wanted this devil to be her friend.

But Francisco merely laughed, low and soft in his throat. 'I have you with me now. I don't let go. Will you remember that?'

He traced the outline of her full lips with a trailing finger and she closed her eyes, shuddering with sensation. Oh, God, she didn't think she could bear it—loving him, wanting him, all so desperately! And his feathery touch was dark magic, a prelude to the mystery of human desire; her lips quivered helplessly, her bones shaking inside her. She didn't know how she could fight it.

Then she heard his almost silent sigh, felt him move away, and opened her drugged eyes, her lids feeling incredibly heavy, to watch him retrieve her hat from where it had fallen in the short, springy grass.

'There,' he said, fitting it on her bright head. 'You will walk with me while I think. Come!'

Just like that, she thought, watching him pluck the haversack from the ground and swing the strap over his shoulder. All that Spanish arrogance was well and truly back in place.

Despite everything, all her attempted commonsense strictures, it made her smile. Made her happy, almost carefree, as she hurried to catch up with his long, loping stride. If walking and thinking was all he now had in mind, she could cope with that. She would enjoy the sense of freedom, of seemingly limitless space. Enjoy it to the full, treasure it, because this was going to be all she would allow herself to have. It was something she could cope with without damaging herself irrevocably.

Somehow or other she was going to have to armour herself against him, control and tame the wild needs which he alone could awaken.

Talking herself into a sensible frame of mind, she was hardly aware of his continuing silence as they trekked along the rocky heights. His profile was harshly austere in the unforgiving rays of the sun and his thoughts had taken him away. He had probably forgotten she was with him.

But that didn't matter. She would never feel alone while he was near. Briskly she slapped that counter-productive thought down and made herself take a guess at the distance they'd covered.

Miles.

And they would have to retrace their steps, and she would probably die of heat exhaustion and de-hydration along the way. If she asked whether there was any coffee left in that flask, would he even bother to answer?

Working up a strong feeling of resentment was certainly helping to block out all those other dead-end thoughts but when he plunged on to a path that led down a deep ravine and turned, holding both hands out to help her, she put her hands trust-ingly into his and knew that nothing on earth could armour her against what he made her feel. Her folly made her want to cry.

He swung her effortlessly down the steepest part of the track and she heaved a great sigh. She was no quitter; she was just going to have to try harder to block him out. She could do it, given time. Then he caught her to him, steering her out of the way of a group of prickly pears, pushing a strand of damp hair back from her hot forehead, telling her, 'Not long now and then you can catch your breath. It is not my intention to exhaust you.'

She pulled away, trying to look as if she couldn't give a damn what his intentions were. But her mind was jumping about in a frenzy. Was he merely being polite? Feeling guilty because she was unused to this kind of terrain and he'd forgotten she was with him? Or was he speaking the truth because he wouldn't want an exhausted woman in his bed tonight?

Her common sense wasn't up to dealing with that so she asked in a rush, 'Not long to what?'

In answer, he pulled her round, pointing further down the mountainside where herds of goats were grazing on the scrub, and further still to where a small hut-like stone building lay in the shade of stunted olive trees. A curl of thin blue smoke rose from the single squat chimney and even as she focused she saw the bent figure of an old man emerge from the shade.

'*El pastor*,' he said softly, the austerity she'd noted earlier leaching from his features. 'He will welcome us to his home and there you will rest your aching feet for a few moments and drink the finest spring water you have ever tasted.'

'He lives there?' Sarah could hardly believe it. There was nothing for miles but the ferocious mountain landscape. 'Doesn't he get lonely? Surely he goes back to the village during the winter?'

'No. He prefers solitude.' Francisco loped down the steep, narrow track, taking one of her hands firmly in his. 'He doesn't like people, generally speaking. He never married and when his mother died, twenty years ago, he moved up here. He tends the goats for the villagers and in return they make payment in vegetables, cheese, the occasional fowl. I usually check up on him once a month at least, more often in the winter.'

By now they were slithering across a barrier of scree and Francisco was laughing, his teeth gleaming whitely, as he caught her up in his arms and carried her over the final unstable yards, then deposited her on firm ground. The old man watched, not smiling until they were near enough for him to reach out and take Francisco's hand. And although the smile looked rarely used there was deep respect in it, and gratitude too, when a packet of tobacco was produced from the haversack, then the rest of the ham, a great lump of cheese wrapped in cool leaves and enough fruit to keep the old man going for a week.

The remains of their picnic, she recognised. They had eaten very little; they had been diverted... Frowning, she pushed that memory away and, annoyingly, her stomach chose that moment to rumble. She didn't begrudge the reclusive goatherd so much as a single grape. Relying, as he seemed to have chosen to do, on the handouts from others, he must sometimes go hungry, she thought compassionately. But she did wonder how she was going to trudge all those miles back on an empty stomach.

Good for the figure, she told herself bracingly as the two men conversed in rapid Spanish, the old man's voice sounding rusty. And then Francisco placed a hand in the small of her back, guiding her to a wooden bench leaning against the stone hut in the shade of the trees, and the goatherd disappeared inside to emerge moments later with two glasses of the coolest, best-tasting water she had ever been offered. It slid down her parched throat like a dream and she was still sipping when a sleek black dog came out of the little house to be fed with chunks of cheese and slices of ham from their picnic.

'So he does have a friend; I'm glad of that,' Sarah murmured while this was going on, and Francisco shrugged eloquently.

'He has many friends, even if he doesn't know it. People from the village, workers on my estates—very few days pass without someone making the journey to see that all is well with him.' He turned to the shepherd, spoke in Spanish, then told Sarah, 'We will go now. We will not outstay our welcome. He has too much courtesy to ask anyone to leave, but he is happier alone.'

He tugged her to her feet, with a few more parting words, then led her into a yard of sorts where an almost brand-new four-wheel-drive vehicle glittered in the sunlight. He opened the passenger door and Sarah questioned, 'What are you doing? Is this his?'

'I made it available to him twelve months ago. So far he has used it only once. His dog cut a paw and it wouldn't heal. He drove it to the vet for treatment.' While she was digesting that he walked round to the driver's seat, telling her, 'I asked if I could borrow it. You have walked far enough. It will be returned to him in the morning.' He flashed her that sudden, irresistible smile. 'We must simply hope that his dog won't injure itself in the meantime.'

She gave him a wavery smile back then stared blindly out of the windscreen. There was a lump in her throat, like a rock. For all his thoughtfulness in borrowing the vehicle she would rather have walked back with him, over the mountain, empty stomach, tired feet and all. She didn't want their outing to end. Once back at the castle she would have to start remembering that she was his captive, start verbally fighting him again.

The rough track led downwards, dust and stones flying beneath the wheels, and eventually ended in a crossroads of sorts.

'Left takes us further into the estates, straight on leads down to the village, right goes back to my home.' He turned briefly, one dark brow questioning. 'You would like to see the village?' And, without waiting for her answer, he drove straight on.

A sudden spurt of excitement brought a huge smile to her face. She erased it swiftly. OK, OK, so she was glad the outing was to be extended, that she was to be given a little more time with the man she had idiotically fallen in love with, just an hour or so more before they must return to being captive and captor. But that didn't mean she could let herself feel quite so gloriously happy.

He was an unsettling man and he had unsettled her, she informed herself, her eyes on the passing scenery which was becoming less harsh with every metre of the steep, tortuously twisting road. And that was not to be marvelled at, given what she'd been through since leaving London. Little wonder

she was unsettled enough to imagine that she'd
fallen in love with him. Wasn't it common knowledge that prisoners formed a special kind of bond
with their captors? And if the man who'd done the
capturing was as drop-dead handsome, as powerful,
as sexually exciting and downright intriguing as
Francisco, then she could be excused for the
ephemeral insanity of imagining love had anything
to do with anything.

As soon as she was on the plane back to London
he would become no more than the irritating
memory of an arrogant, wrong-minded brute who
had stolen time out of her busy, rewarding and suc-
cessful life.

Having reached that deeply gratifying conclusion, she was able to relax in her seat and enjoy
his commentary on what they were seeing as every
twist and turn in the narrow road took them further
down into the fertile river valley.

The rich acres of cereals, the peach orchards, the
olive and citrus groves made fecund patterns across
the land, and the lush greenery of oaks and elms
made a band of speckled shade along the edges of
the river. In the shade of the riverbank he parked
the Jeep, and she looked at the cool sparkling water
and admitted, 'It's all so lovely.'

'More lovely than the mountains and my home?'
He turned, his hands on the wheel, his look intent,
and she shook her head, smiling.

'No. Just different.'

'You like my homeland? What you have seen of
it? If circumstances were different, would you be
happy here?'

'Who wouldn't be?' she evaded, wondering why he was asking, refusing to allow herself inwardly to admit that she would be happy anywhere if she could be with him. Thankfully, he seemed content with her answer, swinging out of the Jeep and helping her down, taking her hand and leading her back on to the road. In moments they were entering the village, a maze of narrow streets, the clean façades of the houses decorated with window-boxes brimming over with geraniums, the tiny gardens awash with roses, honeysuckle and lilies, the walls dripping with purple and scarlet bougainvillaea.

Entering the small cobbled square, she tried to reclaim her hand but succeeded only in making him tighten his grip so tried instead to ignore the warmth of his touch, the sweet sensations that rippled through her body, weakening her until all she wanted to do was cling to him, hold him, never let him go.

Not easy, and not helped by the fact that people went out of their way to greet him. Old men engrossed in animated conversation on the benches facing the central stone fountain ambled over to pass a word or two; young mothers with push-chairs and elderly black-clad matrons who popped out of doorways all addressed him as *patrón*. Wide smiles of pleasure cracked their faces, smiles for her too, and little sidelong glances, weighing up the suitability of *el patrón's* new lady.

Sarah didn't blame them for being curious but she could have done without it. She wasn't his lady, despite the way he had now draped a possessive arm around her shoulders, pulling her close, their bodies touching, presenting them as an item. It was a lie, a sham, yet she had almost been his, up there, high in the mountains. She blushed uncontrollably as her body shuddered with yearning for what had almost been and now must never be, and Francisco gave her a quick look of concern and announced, 'We will eat. Forgive me, you must be hungry. We barely made a dent in the lavish picnic Rosalia provided.'

He dropped a swift kiss on her hectic cheek, said something in Spanish to the growing group of interested villagers, something which raised a gale of laughter, and compounded the felony by telling her, 'We had other things on our minds, didn't we, *querida*?'

Sarah stiffened indignantly. Snake! He didn't have to go out of his way to remind her of what had happened, her out-of-control response to him, the calculated way he had called a halt, did he? And what had he said to all those people that was so darned funny? One thing was certain: he might be the big man around here, rotten rich and lord of all he surveyed, but he was no gentleman!

Anger fuelled by acute embarrassment helped her to shrug his arm from her shoulders as she straightened her spine, telling him frostily, 'I'm capable of waiting until I get back to prison. I won't starve,' and felt better after that, more in control, because it was a timely reminder of how she'd come to be here in the first place, knocking her feeble pretence that this was somehow a day out of time firmly on the head.

He dipped his dark head close to her ear and murmured, 'Sheathe those claws, little cat. You no longer need them,' then took her hand again, led her to a table outside a café and sat her down in the shade of an orange tree. He gave his order and then proceeded to explain how he'd put the fortune he'd made on the world's money markets to good use, providing better amenities for the villagers, making them proud again of the productive estates, and how he'd watched their contentment grow with the betterment of their living conditions.

'You may think it feudal, but it works for everyone,' he told her as he refilled their glasses from the bottle of rich local wine. 'Everything had been neglected—the water supply was erratic, the houses crumbling, little work was done on the estates because what was the use when the produce wasn't harvested at the right time, sold at the right time and at the right price through lack of my ancestor's interest? We are a very isolated community; we have to pull together, all of us, work hard together to survive, to become a viable entity, to prevent the village falling into decay, the land losing its fertility, the lifeblood—the people— moving away to find a decent standard of living somewhere else.' He visibly reined in his enthusiasm, giving her an underbrow look. 'But I am boring you?'

'Far from it,' she denied quickly. But in a way she wished he had been. It would have been easier. But he'd held her interest completely and she knew now why everyone who'd gone out of his or her way to greet him had looked at him with respect and affection.

And far from boasting about what he had achieved she had read the pride in his voice, pride for the workers who had helped him realise his dream, seen the passionate love of his land in his eyes. And she knew she was coming dangerously close to admitting that what she felt for him was neither lust nor the fantasy of imagined love; it was real and abiding and, because of that, grotesquely painful.

'I am glad,' he said simply, standing up as he put down the pesetas to cover the bill. He held out a hand to her, but she wisely ignored it, giving him a tight-lipped nod of agreement as he suggested, 'Shall we go?'

The afternoon was well advanced and there were few people around to waylay them as they walked back through the shimmering heat to where the Jeep was parked. Francisco said little and she said nothing, too busy with her thoughts. And they weren't comfortable companions. Every time she started to congratulate herself for having reached the sensible conclusion that the circumstances, the situation, were responsible for the juvenile way she'd imagined herself in love with him, he upped and did or said something that made her believe that what she felt for him was no fantasy at all.

She was right in the middle of drumming into her head the sheer, self-destructive folly of allowing herself any emotions at all where he was concerned, reminding herself what a lawless brute he was, when he said gently, 'We'll relax, sit in the shade for a while. We can tackle the drive back later, when it's cooler. You must be sleepy.'

She was, she recognised. Suddenly very sleepy. All that fresh air, the exercise, was finally getting to her. Plus the wine she'd had with lunch—and what a lunch! *Pollo a la andaluza*, Francisco had told her as she'd eaten heartily of the delicious chicken with sherry, saffron, almonds and garlic presented in a thick earthenware bowl, with a crisp salad on the side and a dish of roast sweet peppers to dip into. She had been groaningly hungry and couldn't remember ever having eaten so much at one sitting before.

And the shade of the riverbank did look inviting and the idea of bouncing around in the Jeep with such a full tummy didn't really appeal, and if he didn't get too close then she didn't see why they shouldn't cool down in the shade, enjoy the slight breeze that came off the river.

If the time hadn't been right up on the mountains, where there hadn't been another living soul for miles, then he would hardly deem the riverbank a suitable setting for seduction when workers moving to or from the fields might pass by at any time, she rationalised. And took the risk.

'Just for a few minutes,' she agreed, her mouth consciously prim as she wandered nearer to the water's edge and sank down gratefully on the soft green grass. Then she went rigidly still as she heard the unmistakable sound of rustling clothing and turned her head, suspicion sharpening her brilliant eyes.

He had removed his shirt. Her mouth went dry as her eyes were held by his hard, virile body, the smooth olive skin that glistened over wide shoulders and the taut muscles of his flat stomach. She tried to look away but her eyes wouldn't let her; she tried to stand, to walk back to the Jeep and sit in it until he agreed to drive her back but her legs wouldn't move.

He was coming towards her, the discarded shirt
in his hands, and there was unrestrained virile
splendour in the way he moved, sweet dark honey
in his smile, and she laved her dry lips with her
tongue, silently cursing the way her suddenly trembling body had divorced itself from her brain.

He said, with a tiny hint of mockery, 'Relax. It
is siesta time. Use my shirt as a pillow; the rug in
the back of the Jeep probably smells of dog.' Then
he wandered away, arrogant confidence in every line
of his body, and she folded the garment he'd tossed
to her, her fingers shaking.

He had the ability to make such a fool of her,
she thought miserably, watching as he sat down on
the grass half a dozen yards away, his elbows on
his knees, his hands cupping his chin, apparently
lost in contemplation of the gently swirling water.

His timing was positively machiavellian. He
couldn't have failed to see the way she'd been
transfixed by his near-nakedness, her eyes coveting
his gorgeous body; he must have been laughing at
her inside his head, tormenting her with what he
withheld, remembering her 'generous' passionate
response to his earlier, idly experimental love-
making!

She ground her teeth together. She hated and
loathed him, she really did! And that was a whole
load better than imagining herself in love with the
louse! Snorting to herself, she decided she might as
well make use of his wretched shirt and, turning
her back very decisively on him, bunched the soft
fabric under her head. She listened to the music of
the water, to the breeze as it danced through the

tops of the trees and drifted to sleep with her fingers possessively clutching her makeshift pillow.

She woke, disorientated, to find him sitting beside her. It was cooler, the light much dimmer beneath the trees now, and she saw him turn his head to look down at her, his face shadowed, mysterious.

'You slept for three hours.'

A gentle hand brushed the tousled hair away from her face and she struggled upright, objecting blearily, 'You should have woken me ages ago. I'm sorry.'

'It's not important. There's no hurry. And I've been thinking—I want to ask you something, Salome.'

Oddly enough, she couldn't object to that once hated name but reached for his shirt and pushed it at him. There was only so much she could take. She twisted her legs beneath her, not looking at him as he pushed his arms into the sleeves, doing her best to sound reasonably friendly but cool as she invited, 'Ask away.'

She held her breath as he began bluntly, 'Did you mean it when you said I was responsible for the way Encarnación has rejected her home, the values that were instilled into her since birth? It has been plaguing me; I have thought of little else.'

How to answer? The tension coming from him was stinging. He had obviously taken her words deeply to heart and much as a part of her weakly wanted to reassure him, stop him from blaming himself, she knew she could never lie to him again.

'I think it's a distinct possibility,' she answered quietly. 'I don't know her, of course, or what kind of life she had here, but generally speaking the young are curious, adventurous. If freedom to satisfy their curiosity is denied them then sooner or later they'll kick against the traces. I'm not saying that's what happened in your sister's case,' she said into the deep silence. 'Only that it's a possibility.'

'It's more than that,' he said heavily. 'You made me think, made me look at myself. I kept her in a silken cage and when she showed signs of restlessness I thought I could cure it by taking her to Seville, pushing money at her so that she could indulge her passion for beautiful clothes.'

He took her hands in his and she hadn't the power to pull away from the magic of his touch. He needed to talk this out, and she needed to listen, to help if she could, so she told him gently, 'I'm sure you always did what you thought best for her. Teenagers are notoriously hard to handle.'

'Not Encarnación,' he denied bleakly. 'She was always biddable, even as a baby. Too biddable, perhaps. Even when she told me she wished to study art, to make it her career, she did no more than dip her head when I told her I didn't think it suitable, that, being who she is, she didn't need a career.

'I was afraid for her,' he admitted. 'She would have had to live away from home, attend a college where she would have to mix with students who might be on drugs, lead promiscuous lifestyles. I offered to arrange for a private tutor to work with her here, but she declined.'

He sighed deeply. 'Her nature is so gentle and sweet that it was an easy matter for her mother, and then me, to push her into the mould we had decided was suitable. I should have trusted her, allowed her to make some decisions about her own life.'

'Then you can tell her so, when you see her,' Sarah said firmly. 'After all, Spain has emerged from the days when daughters and sisters were kept behind iron grilles.'

'You must think me a tyrant, rooted in the past.' His teeth gleamed in the dusk, his smile bleak. 'There were circumstances——' She watched his shoulders lift in a graceful shrug. 'Our mother came from Aragon, from a great military family, stiffnecked with pride. One summer, long ago, she came south to stay with cousins while she was recuperating from an illness. She met my father and immediately fell in love with him. And he with her. They eloped and she was disowned.

'He was a gypsy, you see. Untamed, even though he had got out of the warren of caves and tunnels above Granada where the children run like a pack of young wolves, swift and tricky and without hope. He got himself out of there by the power of his looks and his voice. As a *cante jondo* singer he was regarded as one of the best in living memory, much in demand for parties given by the wealthy. That is how she met him.'

His lean hands tightened around hers, his thumbs softly stroking her skin. 'After they were married, they lived in a small rented house in Cadiz, managing on what earnings he didn't squander away. When I was five years old he disappeared. He was wild, that one, untamed. The restrictions of a wife and a child and a settled home became too much for him to take. I missed him deeply. He had been my hero—handsome, proud, generous to a fault when he had money, carelessly optimistic when he had none. Laughing or scowling, he drew people to him like a magnet. He made me proud to be part gypsy.'

'Did you never see him again?' she asked gently, hurting inside for the small boy who had watched for the idolised father who had never come home.

Her compassionate heart twisted inside her when he answered sadly, 'Many years later. I was then seventeen. And in the intervening years, believing the wild gypsy had left our lives, my mother's family had unbent sufficiently to make her an allowance, enough to get me a good schooling, had provided a better house in a more acceptable area. And with the unthinking arrogance of youth I let him know he wasn't welcome. We managed without him, he had deserted us once and we didn't want him now. Soon after, he left, and in the fullness of time Encarnación was born. I hated my father then, with all the savagery of blind youth. Can you understand that?'

She nodded mutely, sensing his torment, but he said harshly, 'I can't, not now. In my arrogance I took on the role of my mother's protector, turning him away. If it hadn't been for my rigid attitude they could have had many happy years together. He was older, mellower, and they loved each other. I knew nothing of the blind passion that can pull two people together against all reason.

'That was my first mistake,' he told her bleakly. 'My second was to go along with my mother when she announced that my baby sister must be protected, watched over to make sure that she didn't ruin her life as she herself had done. By that time, the two old aunts who were all that was then left of my mother's family had withdrawn their grudging support. The evidence that she had taken that wild gypsy back into her bed, if only for a few nights, was more than they could bear. So I worked like a mad dog, used my brain to exploit the money markets, became more ruthless than I like to remember. But it meant that my small family could live in comfort, hold their heads up in the community.

'And then I inherited the estates, and the rest you know, and perhaps my biggest mistake of all was when I continued to protect and isolate Encarnación from any possible contamination after our mother's death. It had become a habit. Which is no excuse and doesn't alter the fact that I am to blame for driving her away to God knows what!'

He released her hands and jerked to his feet as if he could no longer contain his regret and pain, and Sarah scrambled up, unable to watch the torment he was putting himself through yet respecting the innate honesty of this proud man, an honesty that had made him ask questions of himself, made him face the unwelcome answers squarely.

She said, 'Don't!' and reached out to touch him, laying her hand against the side of his face. She knew that she loved him, and always would, and would find the strength from somewhere to face the fact that he would never love her. 'Everyone makes mistakes,' she told him gently, knowing her heart was in her eyes. 'We would hardly be human if we didn't. You, at least, have the courage to admit yours. And in your sister's case you can put it right.'

He slid his hands around her waist and she saw the gleam of his smile in the star-spangled purple dusk; she knew that if he wanted to make love to her now she would give herself as generously as she knew how. She desperately wanted to give him whatever comfort she could.

'As soon as I see her,' he promised.

'Before or after you've killed my father?' she chided, unable to resist the temptation, and he pulled her into his arms, holding her so possessively that she thought he'd never let her go.

But he proved her wrong as he released her, keeping a careful distance between them as he told her, 'There is one more thing to say before I take you back. You are free to leave. You were right. I am as unprincipled as your father. I am going to have to try very hard not to be, I think. To that great end I shall not harm a hair of the reprobate's head. I am as much to blame as he for what happened. I will even confess to keeping you in my bed under false pretences. You have too strong a character to even think of jumping from a great height. I followed your pattering feet to the roof because I was curious—I'd heard you huffing and sighing in the bathroom for what seemed like hours.

'I must admit, when I saw you leaning so far over the battlements, I had some fear and rushed to grab you back in case of an accident. But oh, Salome, when you tried to convince me that you had about as much strength of character as a jelly, I couldn't resist pretending to believe you would kill yourself rather than endure my home and me for a moment longer.'

The laughter in his voice curled round her and because she knew she loved him to distraction she couldn't be even slightly annoyed at the way he'd seen through her plots and plans and used them for his own amusement. And anyway, he had said she was free to go, and the thought of leaving, never seeing him again, was a misery that was almost too great to contain.

He escorted her to the Jeep, helped her into the cab and while she waited for him to join her she thought, So that's it, is it? Everything nicely sorted. If the home truths she'd hurled at him—responsible for his black mood of the night before—would help him reach a better understanding with his sister in the future, let Piers off the hook, then fine. She was glad. But where did that leave her?

With her freedom, she supposed numbly. The freedom she'd been fighting and scheming for from the moment he'd shown her into that suite of rooms and locked the door. But London, her work, her neat and comfortable flat seemed like a prison from where she was standing. She didn't want it. She wanted him!

She then got exactly what she'd thought she wanted when he climbed in beside her, started the engine but left it idling, telling her over the rumble, no trace of mockery in that dark velvet voice now, 'You are free to leave in the morning. But I want you to stay. For as long as you like. I need you, as I've never needed anyone or anything. Take an extended holiday; fax Jenny tomorrow. Be my woman. I will sleep in one of the guest rooms tonight—I want to give you that much time to make up your mind. When you share my bed again it will be because that is what you want too.'

CHAPTER ELEVEN

BY THE time they left the Jeep in the castle courtyard Sarah had made up her mind. She didn't need to sleep on it.

She loved Francisco so much it hurt and although he had said nothing about loving her—in fact, it had probably never entered his head—he had said he needed her. So she would stay, partly because he did need her at the moment and partly because she needed him more than he would ever know.

The feelings she had for him went too deep to be denied. And when she left for England she would be leaving him; she was far too level-headed to imagine any other scenario—such as Francisco declaring his undying love, begging her to be his wife.

It was unthinkable. When he decided to marry he would choose a compatriot, a well-connected, upper-class raving beauty, not an unremarkable foreigner who had to work damned hard for her living, whose only family happened to be an old reprobate who regularly earned himself embarrassing publicity in the sleazier of the tabloids.

At the moment he desired her, she accepted that. And the way he had opened up to her about what had happened in the past, laid his guilt over Encarnación on the line, meant that for a time there would be an inevitable closeness between them.

But he would work his way through that, and could even come to resent her for being the recipient of his private anguish over the way he had been instrumental in sending his father away for that second and final time, the part he had unwittingly played in his sister's rebellion. He was proud and he was arrogant and knowing he had allowed her to see him at his most vulnerable would be a cause of acute discomfort. And anyway, by then he would have slaked his desire for her, become bored, wanting her gone because her presence would have become an irritant, an embarrassment probably.

But she could stay for a little while, just a week, and take off before he had a chance to grow tired of her, began to regret ever having bared his soul to her. That way she would have beautiful memories, and because she knew she would love him until the end of her life that wasn't too much to ask for, was it?

No, she had no illusions about this. When she went she would be leaving him for good. And that would be drenchingly painful and the sorrow of it would be with her for a long time to come. But she would have her memories, and in time the pain of it would ease and she would be left with the loveliness of the beautiful days and nights they had shared.

There was no need to waste precious hours pretending to think it over. Her mind was made up. She would tell him now. At least he hadn't tried to pressure her during the journey; he'd stayed silent, leaving her to her own thoughts. She was grateful for that.

He reached for her hand in the darkness as they walked slowly across the huge courtyard to the castle which, in Sarah's loving eyes, now took on the misty aspect of a fairy-tale come true, a place she could grow to love and cherish. But there wouldn't be time for all this to take a stranglehold on her heart and mind. His invitation to stay had carried a limit of a couple of weeks, she made herself remember. Besides, she had promised herself one week only.

His fingers closed reassuringly around hers and her love for him nearly exploded inside her, the sheer enormity of the emotion making her feel faint. But she mustn't give him the slightest inkling of how she really felt. When they parted she didn't want to give him an extra burden of guilt to carry. It would be difficult to hide her true feelings, but she would manage it.

Making her voice cool and light, as if this sort of thing happened to her all the time, she told him, 'About your invitation to stay on for a while—I don't need to think about it; I——'

And then all hell seemed to break loose. The heavy front door was dragged open, light spilling out into the darkness, and a long-legged whirlwind rushed out and hurled itself at Francisco.

Encarnación. It couldn't be anyone else, Sarah decided, stepping back quickly, out of the way, as the tall Spaniard gathered the girl into his arms, returning her bear-hug. Glossy dark hair was re-strained in a thick braid that reached down to her waist and her generously proportioned body was clad in—of all things—the despised blue jeans and sloppy T-shirt. And she was talking non-stop—ex-plaining?—in a torrent of rapid Spanish, her words seeming to fall all over themselves as if she couldn't wait to get them all out.

'Speak English,' Francisco demanded, pleasure and relief enriching and deepening his voice. 'We have a visitor.' He unwound her arms from around his neck. 'You're strangling me!'

'Oh! Of course!' The Spanish girl twirled round and her eyes were sparkling with merriment, eyes the colour of dark, sweet sherry. She was very lovely, Sarah thought; no wonder Piers had acted out of character and romanced a girl younger than his own daughter. 'You're the one he hijacked! Oh, Francisco!' She launched herself at her brother again, hugging her arms around him. 'You are wicked! Did you keep her locked in the dungeon? Feed her on bread and water?'

The way Francisco had described his sister had made Sarah equate her with a cup of sweet, tepid, milky tea. But now she was bubbling like champagne, so her adventure obviously hadn't done her too much harm. And she was back now, safe and sound by all appearances, and from Francisco's obvious relief and happiness he had forgiven her and would rethink the outdated rules he had made her live by in future. So she should be greatly relieved. Why, then, was her overwhelming feeling one of aching emptiness?

'Behave yourself!' Francisco disentangled himself again and Sarah could sense the effort he was having to make to put on the stern big brother act. 'You went away a meek little angel and return in the guise of a minx. Just because I'm relieved enough to let you get away with it this time, don't think you can put me through that kind of anxiety ever again.'

'I'm sorry.' Encarnación bit her lip. 'I didn't think you would be worried. I was only thinking of what I wanted, and he——'

'Is Bouverie-Scott here?' The sudden frosting of his voice told Sarah that he might have forgiven his sister for the worry and upset she'd caused, blaming himself for driving her away, but he wouldn't so readily forgive Piers for taking advantage of a young girl's natural wish to try her wings.

Encarnación answered quickly, her huge eyes shining, 'Oh, yes! He got your message. He said you were so angry you'd kidnapped his daughter and we must come back to face the music together!'

Sarah shivered. Only a couple of hours ago Francisco had given his word that he wouldn't harm the older man and she didn't doubt him. He was a man who could be trusted to keep his word. But that didn't mean that the coming confrontation would be anything but grossly unpleasant.

'Where is he?' She spoke for the first time, aware that the panicky, shivery feeling inside her made her sound almost aggressive, as if she was blaming the girl for what had happened. And Francisco evidently thought so too, judging by the hard, piercing look she earned herself as Encarnación blithely explained.

'He's waiting in the small *sala*. We didn't know how long you'd be so Rosalia fed us and they're chatting away like old friends now, with the brandy bottle for company!'

That figures, Sarah thought bleakly, forcing herself to trail behind the other two as Francisco took his sister's arm and stalked in through the door. Rosalia was just the motherly, jolly type Piers

normally went for. So why hadn't he stuck to merry
widows and kept his hands off beautiful virgins?

If he'd stuck to the pattern of the last decade and
more, none of this would have happened. She
wouldn't have met Francisco and fallen blindly and
hopelessly in love in the space of a few traumatic
days, and that, at this precise moment, seemed no
bad thing because the way the Spanish devil and
his prodigal sister were an obvious entity, shutting
her out, hurt unbearably. He was acting as if she
didn't exist, as if he'd never opened his heart to
her, shared his feelings of guilt, told her he wanted
her, needed her, asked her to stay...

Her heart was several feet below the soles of her
sensible shoes when she followed them through to
one of the cosy family rooms she'd investigated the
day before. She felt, she recognised sickly, like a
faithful old dog which had been discarded by an
uncaring master but was tagging along anyway.

Rosalia bobbed out, beaming, as they entered and
Piers rose from an armchair at the side of the empty
stone hearth, putting his brandy glass down on a
side-table. He didn't look in the least bit ashamed
of himself, but then he had never been ashamed of
his rumbustious lifestyle and was obviously not
thinking of taking that bad habit on board at his
time of life.

At least he was wearing clean fawn trousers and
although his blue shirt was obviously old and faded
it wasn't too badly crumpled and it wasn't covered
in paint stains. His long hair, grey for a few years
now, was still thick and healthy, tied back at the
nape of his neck with a bootlace, and the tan he'd
acquired made his few wrinkles unimportant and

deepened the colour and brightness of his very blue eyes.

The glance he gave Sarah was comprehensive but brief, and, seemingly satisfied that she wasn't actually dragging a ball and chain behind her, he walked towards Francisco, speaking in fluent but probably very ungrammatical Spanish.

Anger whiplashed through Sarah. She would not be ignored, not by any of them! She refused to behave as if she were a dispensable player in this charade. It was her turn to demand, 'Speak English! I've as much right to know what's been going on as anyone. So don't try to shut me out as if I didn't exist!'

This last had been meant exclusively for Francisco but apparently Piers took it personally, turning to her, his hands outstretched.

'Sal, I'm sorry. You're all right, though, aren't you?' He took her hands and held them tight and Sarah blinked, biting her lip because the way she was feeling she might easily cry and she wasn't going to let herself. Piers actually apologising shook her up. He roistered through life thinking he could do as he pleased, and if people didn't like it then it was their tough luck.

Francisco said darkly, 'Your father was just explaining—quite colourfully, too—exactly what he would do with men who abducted innocent young ladies for their own advantage. A rather hypocritical stance for him to take, in the circumstances, don't you think?'

'Now look here!' Piers growled, but the Spaniard quelled him with an icy glare of intense dislike. Sarah had never seen him look so forbidding and accepted, with an inner shudder, that her father was going to get such a scathing run-down of his character that his ego would be smarting for years.

Instinctively she moved closer to the older man and was astonished when his arm went around her shoulder, as if he actually felt some concern for her, some affection. When she'd been little more than a child she had tried to carry on her mother's efforts to act as a regulator in his life and he'd seemed bewildered by it. He'd packed her off to boarding-school and years later, when she'd decided to go her own way, he'd been relieved. When they had, on occasion, met up he'd seemed wary of her, the time he spent with her never short enough.

She glanced up at him quickly but he was frowning, trying to outglare Francisco, whose withering, contemptuous stare now encompassed her.

Encarnación broke the tension, urging, 'Stop it, both of you! If it weren't for Piers, Francisco, I probably wouldn't have come back for ages. He made me understand how anxious you were, and talked me into coming home when I didn't much want to because I was really enjoying myself and he was teaching me things——'

'Teaching!' Francisco exploded, his face white with rage. 'Is that what you call it?' Sarah had never seen him look so ferocious. Piers deserved what was coming to him, but she shuddered for him all the same. '*Dios*!' His black eyes pounced on his sister, his lips pulled back against his teeth. 'Teaching you what, exactly?'

'How to draw!' Piers snapped. 'What did you think? Though I can guess from what my agent said about your visit, the message you left, the insanity of keeping my daughter hostage.'

After a moment of shivering silence, Francisco turned to his sister.

'Is this true? Do not lie to me.'

'Of course it's true,' Encarnación muttered mutinously. 'You didn't care about what I wanted, so long as I stayed at home and behaved myself. When I told you I wanted to study art and have a career you wouldn't hear of it,' she pouted. 'So when Piers offered me a place at his summer school I took it. He didn't know I'd run away from you, so don't blame him!'

Francisco swung back to Piers, his face taut with strain, and the older man answered with a helpless shrug.

'To put the record straight, I don't go in for seducing schoolgirls. I was sitting outside a café in Seville, sketching——'

'And I went up to him to watch,' Encarnación put in quickly. 'He didn't chat me up, if that's what you think. You were at a business meeting and I'd got bored with shopping, and when I realised I was actually talking to Piers Bouverie-Scott I couldn't believe my luck. When he offered me a place at his summer school—with students from England as well as Spain—I jumped at it. If I'd asked if I could go you wouldn't have let me. I told you who I'd be with in that note. You knew I wanted to study art; you should have made the connection,' she accused sulkily.

'You didn't realise she wasn't free to take up your offer?' Francisco questioned.

Piers looked as if he didn't understand and countered, 'Free? What's freedom got to do with it? Everyone should be able to do what they feel impelled to do. But if you're asking me if I knew she was running away from home, and not telling her family where she'd be, then no, I didn't know that, not until I got your crazy message.' He gave a sudden grin. 'Though not so crazy now I come to think of it—given the reputation I seem to have earned myself.'

Francisco gave him a long, considering look then dragged in a breath through pinched nostrils.

'You have my unreserved apologies, *señor*. You too, *señorita*.' The cold pride in his black eyes froze her and raw apprehension turned her stomach to knots. 'As it's too late for you to leave tonight I'll ask Rosalia to prepare a guest room. She will tell you when it's ready. Now, excuse me, if you will,' he added, very formal, very Spanish in his straight-backed, arrogant dignity. 'My sister and I have many things to discuss.'

Watching him shepherd Encarnación out of the room, Sarah felt ill. So correct, so formal, so politely dismissive of her. The formal *señorita* had said it all. Where had Salome gone? she wondered despairingly.

She knew he had much to discuss with his sister, bridges to mend, a freer future to offer her, but couldn't he have shown her—with a single word or look—that his invitation still stood, that he still needed her?

But perhaps he didn't need her, not any more. His sister was back, piqued but unscathed, and he'd been given a chance to mend his mistakes. So he wouldn't need her body in his bed to divert him from his uneasy feelings of self-blame, make him feel better about himself.

But maybe he did still want her? Maybe, after the heart-to-heart was out of the way, he would come to her, beg her to stay with him——

'I can't tell you how sorry I am that you got involved in all this, though I must admit I wasn't too worried about you. Miles had him rapidly checked out—who and what he was. He's too wealthy and well-respected to do anything to bring his life down in ruins. I knew he wouldn't harm you. I even got to feel sorry for the guy at one stage.' He grinned at her. 'That girl of mine has more prickles than a porcupine and a tongue like a razor, I told Miles. He'll probably put her on the next plane back to England just to get a bit of peace and quiet!'

Piers reclaimed his brandy glass and lifted it. 'Want some?' She shook her head abstractedly and he confided, 'Well, I feel I need it, even if you don't. It's all been a bit of a nightmare. As I said, when Miles phoned, and——'

'He knew where you were, how to contact you?' Sarah asked, her brows knotting together. 'He told me he didn't know where you were, but hinted at Spain.'

She watched her father gulp at his brandy. He looked uncomfortable, and that wasn't like him.

'I forbade him to tell anyone. I'd set up this summer school in an old farmhouse outside Jerez. Fabulous vineyards. Offered tutorials—a kind of

working holiday free of charge to underprivileged
kids who'd be mugging old ladies and stealing cars,
left to their own devices. Most of them hadn't held
a paintbrush since junior school but you'd be surprised what a metaphorical kick up the backside
and a bit of motivation can achieve. Using creative
talents they never knew they had takes their mind
off their problems like you wouldn't believe.

'There's one lad in particular—he'll go far. I'm
in the process of persuading him to let me sponsor
him through college. He comes from a Liverpool
slum and can barely read or write so he thinks he
wouldn't fit in. But I'll twist his arm yet——'

'Dad!' There was a smile in her eyes and a lump
in her throat. She had always been proud of his
genius but was prouder still of the way he had given
his valuable talents, time and energy to helping
those society had rejected, and what Francisco
would think if he ever found out the type of
company his 'princess' had been mixing with didn't
bear thinking about. But, 'Why was I forbidden to
know how to contact you?' she wondered.

'It was strictly off the record,' he said shame-
facedly. 'If it was a success, and it is, it would be
an annual thing. But if it got known I'd come over
as a do-gooder, and that wouldn't suit my image!'

'Dad!' This time there was a definite giggle. 'You
can't possibly like the image you have!'

'Like it?' Blue eyes crinkled. 'I'm proud of it! I
keep all my Press cuttings—the more way-out the
better. They'll be something to amuse me when I'm
ninety, creeping around on my Zimmer-frame!' He
tossed off the remainder of his brandy, then told
her firmly, 'If you ever thought I horsed around

while your mother was alive, forget it. I can't say I haven't looked, but so far I've never found another to come near my Patience. I know you don't approve of me, but——'

He broke off, relief on his face, as Rosalia walked in, speaking to him in Spanish, and he translated, 'My room's ready, it seems. I'll turn in.' He touched the top of her head briefly. 'I'd like to make an early start in the morning—can't have those tearaways missing too many sessions. I can take you to the airport—unless you'd like to spend a day or so with me at the farm?' he suggested warily, as if it was too much to expect.

She said, 'I'll think about it,' because she didn't know yet whether Francisco wanted her to stay.

She took herself off to his suite, her stomach feeling as if it was home to a colony of grasshoppers, and waited for him. She spent ages in the bath, and because she couldn't bear to wear the torn, dull nightie she took a silky robe of Francisco's and wore that instead, cinching her waist with the tie-belt she found in one of the pockets. Then she perched at the head of the bed, waiting, still waiting, tortured by the spicy, tangy male scent of him that came with the soft fabric.

She wished she didn't love him so much that her heart was hurting, her body aching just to be near him, her soul calling out to his. Why didn't he hear it?

At three o'clock she knew the waiting was over. He couldn't have been talking to Encarnación all this time. He was not going to come to her, tell her how his interview with his sister had gone, what had been settled between them, ask her to tell him what she'd decided about staying on with him. She had already told him she'd made up her mind, didn't need to sleep on it. And that, she decided with a misery that overwhelmed her, could mean only one thing.

He had no further interest in her.

Curling herself into a dejected ball, she tried to sleep, but knew she couldn't, and didn't, and got up with the dawn. She dressed in the grey trousers and shirt Rosalia had laundered, dragged her blazer from the wardrobe, stuffed the torn nightdress and spare underwear in her flight bag and walked out of the room without a backward glance.

She would wait in the inner courtyard until Piers was ready to leave. It couldn't be soon enough. And it was all for the best, she assured herself dully. Why get herself more emotionally involved than she already was? It wasn't worth it, not for a few days and nights of bliss with the man she had been crazy enough to fall in love with.

With his sister safely returned to the fold, everything sorted, the last thing he would want would be to have her around, reminding him of yesterday, of things he would now wish unsaid, undone.

And with his kid sister under the same roof he wouldn't want to set a bad example, indulge in a short-lived affair with a woman he would send packing without a moment's regret the moment she began to bore him.

So she would leave with her dignity intact, and no one would ever know that her poor heart was breaking up. As she emerged into the fresh morning light she waited, staring at her feet because she refused to look around her. This was the place of her dreams; everything she held most precious to her was bound up here. She didn't want to add to her burden of memories.

'So. You are leaving.'

She froze, her body rigid, then killed the tiny unbidden hope stone-dead because his voice had held nothing but a cool lack of interest, either way. Forcing herself to turn and face him, she was shocked by what she saw, but wouldn't let herself feel any concern. Any display of emotion, from hereon in, could be her downfall.

He was wearing the same clothes he'd had on yesterday. Hadn't he been to bed at all? He didn't look as if he had. His face looked grey with fatigue, and he needed a shave, and the soft dark hair was rumpled. But his eyes were like stone, the glance he swept over the trousers and shirt he had so deplored faintly contemptuous.

She dropped her eyes, unable to bear his coldness, his cruelty. If he had given her just a hint of a smile, a look that said he still found her desirable, she would have come right out with it and asked if he still wanted her here. But there'd been nothing, and that had to be for the best, in the long run. Then she closed her eyes, pain washing over her, as Piers popped out from nowhere.

The fantasy, for that was all it had ever been, was over.

'Ready, Sal?' Piers sounded full of himself and Sarah managed a wan smile.

'When you are.'

'Then we're off. The minibus is parked out the front. Not luxury travel but useful for ferrying a bunch of students about.' He marched over to Sarah and took her arm. 'We won't hang around for breakfast,' he decided, as if he'd been asked. He gave the bleak-eyed Spaniard a cocky stare. 'What do you think, Sal? Shall we sue the crazy man?'

He seemed to think it was funny and she wanted to scream at him, tell him this wasn't a joke, that she was being torn apart, tell him to get lost, to give her two minutes of privacy to say goodbye to the arrogant black-hearted devil who'd stolen her heart.

But she didn't; of course she didn't. Her eyes fixed on her father, she said brittly, 'I couldn't be bothered. He did provide me with a free holiday of sorts, excellent food and even better wine. He even threw in some vaguely amusing entertainment—when he was in the mood. Let's go, shall we?'

'He's here again!' Jenny practically sang over the internal phone. 'I thought you told me it was just a casual holiday thing. He didn't look casual to me! All dark and brooding and definitely edible! Anyway, I told him to go on through.'

The line went dead, the door opposite her desk bounced open and he was standing there, six feet plus of dark Spanish arrogance, and she knew that the scant two weeks she'd had, including the few days she'd spent at the summer school with Piers and the students, hadn't been nearly enough time to prepare herself for actually having to see him again.

He was wearing a soft-as-butter cream-coloured leather jacket over black shirt and trousers and he shattered every last one of her senses. She supposed, light-headedly, that the English spring would feel positively frigid after the Andalusian heat.

She didn't know what he was doing here. Had he come to torment her? Was he that cruel?

'Say something!' he ordered, his hands planted on his lean hips, his eyes alarming. 'Or have you forgotten your tongue, along with the things I taught you? How to be a real woman, for instance.' He covered the space between the door and her desk in a blink of her startled eyes, snatched at her hands and dragged her to her feet. 'All that beautiful hair scraped back as if you were ashamed of it. A suit that makes you look like a prison warder! I came only just in time. Another day and you would have been set in concrete, a frigid, uptight single lady to the end of your dreary days!'

He had only come to insult her and she couldn't bear it. She didn't want to remember how he'd made her feel—gloriously, wickedly feminine for the very first time. So she wouldn't remember. She shook his hands away, took two paces back, avoiding his impatient eyes, and said coldly, 'What do you want?'

'A wife.'

Piers had been right. He was a crazy man. She took a deep breath, made sure her mind was in full control before she opened her mouth, then snapped out, 'I don't operate a marriage bureau, Señor Casals. I suggest you go and look behind a few aristocratic Spanish grilles.'

'I do not want to look behind anything but your formidable disguise,' he said fiercely. 'And no, of course you don't operate a marriage bureau. You haven't enough romance in your soul!'

Sarah went white. Struggling to contain the wild emotional upheaval that was taking place inside her, she turned and lurched to the window, clutching the sill, staring out blindly at the back of the office premises, seeing nothing but his extravagantly gorgeous face.

How dared he say she had no romance in her soul? How dared he, when her love for him had filled her soul every moment of every day for the last two weeks? When every time she closed her eyes she saw his face? When, in the midst of her restless dreams, in almost every waking moment, she heard his voice?

She had even, God help her, been drawn closer and closer to the idea of selling the agency, taking the money and slinging her hook, trying to find something interesting to do with the rest of her life. Something absorbing enough, challenging enough to block him out. Her agency, once the centre of her existence, meant less than nothing to her now.

Her hands clenched into fists. He had done that to her! He had made her do what she'd determinedly vowed never to do—let her emotions make a mess of her life. And he had the gall to come here, criticise the way she dressed, taunt her with the fact that, at long last, he had decided it was time he took a wife! What did he expect her to do? Applaud?

'You're wasting my time,' she said thinly. The only positive thing to come out of the wild fantasy of those few days in Spain with him was her new and closer relationship with Piers. Everything else was negative. She had to remember that.

Tears choked her throat as she heard him curse colourfully and violently in his own language. He came to stand beside her and as she turned her face away, unable to look at him, fiercely determined that he wouldn't see how easily he could make cry, he scoffed, 'When you live with me, you will not look out on to brick walls and dustbins; you will see the mountains and valleys of the most beautiful, vital country God created.'

He touched her shoulder and she gasped, every atom of her being converging beneath the fire of his fingers. And then the tears really came, pouring down her face, and he put an imperative finger beneath her chin, turning her head, watching the shame of her watery weakness. She gulped, sniffing inelegantly, wishing she could vanish in a puff of smoke because she'd been weak enough, uncontrolled enough, to burst into messy tears and betray herself.

And clearly, from what he had said, he'd decided that he wanted her in his bed after all. For a couple of weeks, as he had so lightly suggested, putting a time limit on her ability to interest him. Which meant that Encarnación wasn't around to be contaminated by big brother's dubious moral example.

Well, she wouldn't oblige! She had insanely believed that the pain would be worth it, for the memories she would be able to store away. She had guessed at, but hadn't then experienced, the agony of being apart from him. Second time round would be impossible to bear, knowing that when he'd got her out of his system he would go on the prowl for a suitable bride.

'So you do have a heart, and it can be broken,' he said cruelly. 'I am pleased. When you said, in that prim little voice, that you'd already made up your mind about staying on with me, your tone, your manner, and the anguish of my own heart, told me that despite responding to me so gloriously you were far too sensible to do anything so rash. I thought then that you didn't have a heart. Only a little black book, full of unbreakable rules.'

He had got it so wrong, she thought shakily, leaning her head weakly against his leather-clad shoulder. He had jumped to the wrong conclusion about her decision and she wasn't going to correct him. And she had no idea why she was doing this, leaning against him, melting into him, allowing him to get away with stealing the pins out of her hair. She should be firmly ordering him out. Threatening to send for the police if he refused to go. Instead . . .

'But still I hoped,' he told her in a voice of monumental suffering, and she permitted herself a wan little smile, hidden in his shirt, because with Francisco Garcia Casals every emotion would be larger than life, every ounce of sensation wrested from it. And pathos was coming in buckets as he sighed, 'I had promised you a night on your own to think things over. For that I deserve praise, this is true. I could have so easily persuaded your body, but I wanted also to persuade your mind. I forbade myself to come to you. I waited the night out, praying to the saints that you would change your mind about leaving, only to find you in the morning, dressed again as Chairman Mao, so eager to leave you could barely speak to me, except to insult me. You implied I'd been nothing more than an amusing entertainment. You anguished me!'

Sarah dragged her lower lip between her teeth. How on earth could he make her want to laugh hysterically when her heart was almost audibly breaking? He was utterly impossible, and his dented ego was making his English quite peculiar.

He had removed all her hairpins, tossing them disdainfully away to the four corners of her office, arranging the loosened, glitteringly pale mass over her shoulders, and now he turned his attention to her face, cupping his hands on either side of her head, forcing her away from the refuge of his now damp shirt.

He said growlingly, 'You make me insane. I had not a thought in my head of taking you hostage until your proper little personage glared at me over this desk. An exquisite beauty dressed as a battle-axe, behaving like a robot. I longed to tear off the disguise and find the real woman. So I did crazy, foolhardy things——'

'Wicked things,' she elaborated sternly, wanted to negate the way he made her feel—weak with love, awash with submissive femininity, hopelessly at sea in an ocean of yearning.

'Of course.' His black eyes glittered. 'With you I will always do wicked things. How can I resist, when you make me do them? The way you schemed to get the better of me amused and intrigued me, made me respond and leap one stride ahead, then wait to see what you would do next to overtake me. And all the time, every second, I was growing more enthralled, hardly able to keep my hands off you, lost in admiration of your body and your brain.

And you said things that made me think, examine myself, and no other person has been able to do that.

'So I did the correct thing. I gave you your freedom,' he concluded with dignified simplicity. 'And, because I suddenly found I couldn't bear the thought of your leaving, I asked you to stay. I was wrong.'

His thumbs stroked her damp eyelids, brushing away the tears that spiked her lashes. 'So many tears,' he breathed, 'give me much hope.'

Her brows peaked, her soft mouth quivering. She wasn't following his line of thought. She whispered shakily, 'What are you saying?'

'I should have known you wouldn't so easily give way to the fires of passion. You had spent all your life pretending they didn't exist. I should have thought of that and given you a little black book full of rules and opt-out clauses and contracts signed with blood, along with my invitation. It was only when I watched you walk away that I knew I wanted nothing to do with opt-out clauses, that I wanted you with me until the end of my life, that I had been falling in love with you.'

Shock rippled through her, making her giddy. She clung to him feverishly, her voice shaky as she demanded, 'Say that again.'

'What, all of it?' His voice was growly with laughter. 'Or just that I love you more than life, want you to be my wife, make you big with my babies?'

'Oh, Francisco,' she breathed deliriously, further speech impossible as his arms closed around her, bringing her up against the demanding thrust of his body, and his mouth covered hers, his lips forcing hers apart with gentle determination. She responded wildly, dazed by the fantasy that had become glorious fact, melting, whimpering with ecstasy as his hands impatiently removed her navy blue structured suit jacket and began undoing the buttons down the front of her neat white blouse.

Only then did the serpent of common sense slide through her frenzied, passionate responses. She took his hands and made them go still, her voice raw with hunger as she reminded him, 'This is my office. Any one of half a dozen people could walk right in!'

'Not so.' Soft black eyes invited her to drown in them. 'I locked the door behind me and dared Jenny to put a call through on pain of her life. And this is not your office,' he denied softly as she reached up to twine her loving fingers through his soft dark hair. 'It is your prison.' He swept a raking, disparaging glance around. 'And it doesn't even have a sofa.' Quick fingers slotted the buttons of her blouse back into their holes. 'I do not make love to my future wife on an office floor.'

He retrieved the jacket he'd tossed aside and gently eased her arms into the sleeves and she bit down on her swollen mouth, trembling now between laughter and passion, as he dictated, 'You will walk out of your prison with me, into the splendid freedom of our future. And you will get rid of it—the agency—everything. It is thriving—I made enquiries—so you will have no difficulty selling it, and none of your employees will need fear for their jobs. *Es verdad*?'

'Did anyone ever tell you what a chauvinistic bully you are?' she asked dreamily as he frowningly tugged at her jacket to make it hang straight, and he lifted his arms and his shoulders in a typically arrogant shrug.

'I wouldn't listen to them if they did, *querida*. How can it be bullying to make the woman I love supremely happy?' Then his eyes glinted warily. 'You want me to make you happy? To be my wife, to live in my land and share my home, my estates? You do love me?'

'Oh, Francisco—deeply, forever—of course I do!' She twined loving arms around his neck and he grinned, nuzzling into her hair, whispering wickednesses, and she shuddered with melting abandonment.

Finally he unwound her arms and said gruffly, 'Why are we waiting? We have our life to begin. Come.' Imperious hands pushed her bag at her as he hustled her out of the room. His arm was firmly around her as they paused in the outer office and he told the grinning Jenny, 'You are now in control here. My future wife——' his smouldering eyes were full of pride as they lingered on Sarah's enraptured face '—will be finding a suitable buyer for the agency, and will increase your salary to compensate for your extra responsibility.'

And before anyone could say anything they were out on the street and into a waiting cab, the meter merrily ticking over. Francisco gave the address of her flat then drew her firmly into his arms, kissing her until her face was hectic with desire. His voice sounded fractured as he whispered, 'We will be on our way to Spain tomorrow, *querida*, where we will be married. Encarnación is waiting eagerly for our arrival, and I have seen Piers and asked him to be on hand to give you away. My sister will be leaving for California after the ceremony. I want only the two of us until our babies arrive.'

'Francisco!' She tipped her head, trying, and failing, to look annoyed. But she was worried. 'You're not actually sending the poor girl away? How could you?'

'You know I'm not such a brute, don't you?' he growled, his eyes dancing. 'No, it is something she wants. After Piers convinced her that her artistic talent was negligible, she decided she would like to become a flying doctor in Australia! When I pointed out the impracticalities of such a thing she agreed to think again.

'And then heaven intervened in the shape of the parents of her best friend at convent school. Ana had been invited to spend twelve months with cousins in California and wanted Encarnación to go with her. Naturally, my little sister jumped at the opportunity and I agreed. It will broaden her life experience and—who knows?—she might find something sensible she wants to do with her life. There were many arrangements to be made; that is why I did not come for you sooner.

'And perhaps,' he suggested almost diffidently, 'before our wedding, you would like Encarnación to take you shopping? Madrid, Seville—even Paris or Rome if you like. She is very good at it.'

Sarah shook her head, revelling in the way he was running his hands through her long bright hair. 'I will need new things,' she agreed huskily, 'but I want you to choose them for me. I want you with me.' Gladly, she resigned herself to a future of being clothed in silk and satin and lace and cottons so delicate and fine you could see your hands through them, her eyes brimming with love as his glowed with satisfaction.

'I am glad. We are as one in all things. My heart dies a little every moment we are apart.'

'Then we will never be apart again, my darling,' she promised, snuggling more deeply into his strong arms, adoration for her gorgeous, arrogant, impossible Spaniard coursing through her veins as he whispered against her mouth,

'Never!'

HARLEQUIN PRESENTS®

It's the wedding of the month!

The latest in our tantalizing new selection of stories...

Wedlocked!

Bonded in matrimony, torn by desire...

Coming next month:

THE BRIDE IN BLUE
by Miranda Lee
Harlequin Presents #1811

The author whom everyone's talking about!

It was Sophia's wedding day, but she wasn't a happy and
radiant bride. How could she be when she wasn't marrying
Godfrey, the father of the baby she was expecting...but his
younger brother instead? Jonathon Parnell was ruthlessly
carrying out the deathbed promise he's made to Godfrey: to
marry Sophia and look after their child. Jonathon claimed
he wanted Sophia only as a wife of convenience, but Sophia
suspected that, actually, Jonathon wanted *her*...

Available in May wherever Harlequin books are sold.

BRIDE'S BAY RESORT

UNLOCK THE DOOR TO GREAT ROMANCE AT BRIDE'S BAY RESORT

Join Harlequin's new across-the-lines series, set in an exclusive hotel on an island off the coast of South Carolina.

Seven of your favorite authors will bring you exciting stories about fascinating heroes and heroines discovering love at Bride's Bay Resort.

Look for these fabulous stories coming to a store near you beginning in January 1996.

Harlequin American Romance #613 in January
Matchmaking Baby by Cathy Gillen Thacker

Harlequin Presents #1794 in February
Indiscretions by Robyn Donald

Harlequin Intrigue #362 in March
Love and Lies by Dawn Stewardson

Harlequin Romance #3404 in April
Make Believe Engagement by Day Leclaire

Harlequin Temptation #588 in May
Stranger in the Night by Roseanne Williams

Harlequin Superromance #695 in June
Married to a Stranger by Connie Bennett

Harlequin Historicals #324 in July
Dulcie's Gift by Ruth Langan

Visit Bride's Bay Resort each month wherever Harlequin books are sold.

HARLEQUIN ®

HARLEQUIN PRESENTS®

—where satisfaction is guaranteed!

Coming next month, two classic stories
by your favorite authors:

FORGOTTEN HUSBAND
by Helen Bianchin
Harlequin Presents #1809

They said he was her husband...

But Elise didn't feel married to Alejandro Santanas, or
the mother of his unborn child. The accident had destroyed
her memory of the past few months. Had she really been in
love with this handsome stranger—and would he expect
that passion again?

ONE NIGHT OF LOVE
by Sally Wentworth
Harlequin Presents #1810

Once bitten, twice shy!

Oliver Balfour was the most attractive man Dyan had ever
met. But she wasn't going to mix business with pleasure.
From experience Dyan knew that a man like Oliver
would stalk a woman like her by lying his way into her
affections...and then go quickly for the kill in her bed!

Harlequin Presents—the best has just gotten better!
Available in May wherever Harlequin books are sold.

TAUTH-8